Beautiful Envy

MUSIC CITY DIARIES

KRIS BUTLER

Beautiful Envy

MUSIC CITY DIARIES

KRIS BUTLER

Contents

I'm on the run once again. But this time, I'm alone.

With nowhere to go and a sadistic madman after me, I escape to the one place no one will ever look for me—my best friend, Lennox's house.

Except she has the opportunity of a lifetime and no matter how envious I am of her, I won't let her throw it away to help me. So I'll go along with Slade's plan to stay with a trusted friend. A friend who happens to be a six-foot bearded ginger covered in tattoos and the Pres of his own MC club—the Brotherhood.

Lennox swears he's different and can protect me, but from what I remember of the man, he's nothing more than an overgrown teddy bear. Yeah, I'm not holding my breath.

Between the other two members of the club, my mission to find Maddox, and push Bubba's buttons every chance I get... Well, I soon become dickupied and forget all my troubles.

But trouble finds me anyway, giving me a choice to make —keep running or rise up.

The only beautiful thing about envy is when you realize it's all right at your fingertips, you just have to be brave enough to grab hold. Are you ready for me boys?

This book is interconnected with the Tattooed Hearts world. There will be some overlap, so like always, reading both will enhance your story experience, but not necessary. This series is a why-choose romance, meaning Darcie will not have to settle for one dessert. This book contains content warnings so please be advised before reading. This story is intended for readers 18+ due to the language and content. This is book 2 of 3.

This is a contemporary why-choose motorcycle club romance intended for 18+ due to language and sexual content. There is no sword crossing in this book. This book deals with some themes that might be triggering to readers. I always make effort to handle things with care for my characters and the reader. So please make sure to take care of yourself first.

This book series is connected to the Tattooed Hearts series. This book series features Darcie, Lennox's friend. If you haven't read Riddled Deceit, Smudged Lines, or Open Road, there might be some small spoilers, but it won't take away your experience reading them or this series.

SOME THINGS TO CONSIDER ARE THE FOLLOWING

From Beautiful Agony:

- Sexual assault, rape
- depression
- self harm

In this book:

- Stalker
- Physical violence
- Attempted kidnapping
- Past sexual abuse
- Gangs/MC clubs
- 'God' used casually or in a sexual context
- Insecurity about not being good enough or enough
- Grief (mom's death, loss of dreams, friends)
- Betrayal from parents (using children for own gain, not standing up for their children)

TROPES, CONTENT, AND WHAT TO EXPECT

- Multi-POV, contemporary, MC Club
- Hurt/comfort

- Found family
- Age Gap
- Grumpy cinnamon roll who tries to hold out
- Sweet Rodeo star cowboy
- Cocky but insecure model/mechanic
- Damaged but dedicated first love/bodyguard
- Dirty talk
- Exhibitionism
- Voyerism
- Threesome
- Possessive and growly men
- All the tattoos
- "Good girl"
- Dominating men
- A Queen rising up

You're a fucking Queen.

Now say it back.

CHAPTER 1

Darcie

LENNOX KEPT her eyes on me, her hand tight in mine as I shared my story. Her face was pained, a tear trickling down her cheek every now and then. She didn't interrupt, letting me get out every detail of my sordid past. With one last breath, I heaved a sigh, my tale coming to a close.

"So, I got into the car and drove. I'm sorry to bring you into this mess, but I didn't know what else to do."

The tears I'd been able to hold back threatened to spill now that I was done. I felt a little lighter, having shared my burden, but my heart was heavy from the emotional toil. I sagged into the couch, too afraid to look at the others.

"Darcie, never apologize for needing a friend. I'm glad you came."

Lennox hugged me, her arms feeling like healing beacons of warmth as she wrapped them around me. The last bit of my restraint broke, my sobs pouring out of me. My body shook with the force of my tears, and I let it all go.

I cried for the girl who hadn't been home in years, whose family had been taken away. I wept for the girl whose first love had to leave her and the hole he left in his wake. And I sobbed for the life I'd finally created for myself and how that was now gone as well.

Nothing in my life ever remained, and I was sick of losing.

That thought sobered me, the tears beginning to dry as I found the strength I'd built begin to return.

I drew back, wiping my eyes, surprised to find a box of tissues in front of my face. Glancing up, I spotted Simon holding them out to me.

"Thank you," I sniffled, taking the box and pulling a few free to wipe my eyes and blow my nose. It wasn't a pretty task, but I felt better once it was done.

"We should tell my dad," Lennox said, nodding to herself.

"I'm not sure that's the right call in this situation, Peach," Slade said from behind me. I turned, taking in his tense posture against the wall.

Lennox slumped, her shoulders dropping at his words. "I... I'm not sure what to do then. Especially with..." she trailed off, her eyes staying on her hands as she twisted in her lap.

"What is it, Len?" I asked, worried I'd dumped too much on her plate.

She looked up, her face changing as she made up her mind about something. "It's nothing. You can stay here as long as you need to, Darcie. I'll help you, however I can."

"Peach," Slade growled, but she ignored him, some of her fire returning.

"What isn't she telling me?" I asked the guys, glancing around. Slade was busy staring down Lennox, who avoided his gaze. Simon wore a sheepish grin but didn't say anything. It was Thane who filled me in when I met his eyes.

"She got asked to go on tour with Shadows of Mayhem. We leave in the morning."

"Shut up! That's amazing, Len!" I shouted, reaching over to hug her. She tensed but accepted my embrace.

Through my happiness for her, I finally understood what was going on.

"You have to go," I said, drawing back. "This is a once-in-a-lifetime opportunity."

"There will be others. Plus, you need me. I'm your friend, and I'm choosing to help you instead."

I smiled at her, loving this girl in front of me even more. She truly was one of a kind.

"And that's exactly why I can't let you pass on this opportunity. You're amazing, Lennox, and everyone deserves to know that. If I can just stay here tonight, I'll figure something out. You don't need to reroute your life for me."

She started to protest when Slade spoke up, her mouth closing.

"I might have another solution to offer," he said, his deep voice brokering no arguments.

"You could come with us!" Lennox yelled, a smile spreading across her face.

The thought of being stuck in a vehicle with my bestie and her three boyfriends sounded as appealing as a bikini wax. I grimaced, hoping that wasn't what Slade had in mind.

"Um," I hedged, turning to him, urging him to tell me something different.

He was watching Lennox, a soft smile on his face for her. When he turned to me, the softness was gone, and the no-nonsense man I'd come to know had returned.

"As fun as that would be," he started, making my heart race; he was going to agree with her, "it wouldn't be the wisest or safest option for either of you. Plus, I doubt your bestie wants to be there for our after-concert celebrations."

Lennox's face heated, and she squirmed in her seat. "Okay, what's this brilliant plan then?" she asked, crossing her arms in a defensive pose. I saw through it, though, and knew it was more likely she was turned on and didn't want me to know.

"Bubba," Slade said, not giving any other explanation.

Lennox's face lit up at the name, her eyes sweeping

back and forth as she thought about it. Her smile widened as she nodded.

"Oh, yes. That's perfect. Bubba will know how to protect you. He's part of your world."

"My world?" I asked, lifting my eyebrow incredulously. I'd met the man once and didn't know how the oversized teddy bear was supposed to protect me.

"He's the leader of the Brotherhood."

She said it like I should know it, but I'd never heard of the Brotherhood before. I shook my head, not understanding what she was trying to tell me.

"He's a biker, but it's not like you're thinking," Slade said, eying Lennox. "His club isn't what you're used to. But Lennox is right that he knows your world. He's the best one I can think of to protect you. I'd trust Lennox with him," he added, letting me know how much he thought of this man.

"I don't know. Maybe I should just keep going in the morning. I need to check on someone anyway," I mumbled. The thought of putting my faith in a strange man's hands I'd met once felt scary. Especially if he was a biker. I wasn't sure I trusted anyone in that world outside of Maddox.

Thinking of him brought a pang of sadness, the tears threatening to spill again. I missed him. I needed him. And he wasn't here. Again.

I prayed what Chase said was true, despite the fact that it meant Maddox was in jail. The thought of him purposefully staying away hurt too much. The message

Chase wanted me to give him roared to the surface, and I knew I needed to find him. I needed to make sure his sister was safe. Maddox would want that. It gave me something other than myself to focus on too.

"If you won't stay with Bubba, I won't go on my tour. It's as simple as that, Darce," Lennox said.

"What?" I practically shouted, my heart beginning to race. "That's not fair. He's practically a stranger!"

"You asked us for help, and this is us helping. If you trust me, then trust that I wouldn't put you in more danger. I promise. This could be the perfect place for you to hide and lie low. No one will expect it. I'll be on the road, creating some distance as well. You won't be safe anywhere else, and you know it."

She had a point, but I didn't want to admit it. Staying with someone new would keep me more hidden, especially if she was out on tour. If no one was after me, I would have the time I needed to develop a plan. Their idea had the potential to keep us both safe. Plus, I knew Slade would never jeopardize Lennox's safety after the incident with the stalker, so I had to take his word that this guy was okay.

Sighing, I dropped my head, nodding. I didn't have it in me to say the words.

"Let's get you cleaned up and into bed. It's been a long night. In the morning, we'll talk with Bubba. It's going to be okay, Darce," Lennox soothed, taking my hands and pulling me from the couch.

I didn't know if I believed her words, but I wanted to

trust her. It was hard to have faith in good things when everything was falling apart.

She ushered me into a shower, turned on the water, and showed me where Simon kept his best products. When the steam billowed out of the curtain, she hugged me tight and kissed my cheek, saying she'd be back later to check on me.

Nodding, I stripped out of my clothes and numbly stepped into the water. I felt it hit my skin, but outside of the pressure, I was unaware of my surroundings. My brain was officially going offline, having dealt with too much already. Now that I was relatively safe, the fight-or-flight part was deactivating, leaving me a numbed-out mess.

Going through the familiar motions, I washed my body. When I spotted a hint of red in the water around my feet, my memories surged up, and I remembered what brought me here.

Chase.

I'd killed him.

Or at least I thought I had. It was all a blur at the end as my need to get out of there surged through me.

The feel of the knife as I shoved it into him and the slipperiness of the blood were all I could focus on. Everything else was a haze as I tried to recall if he had a heartbeat or seemed coherent when I left.

I didn't know if I wished him dead or alive. Both had a series of consequences attached to them. Neither were things I could solve at this moment.

Scrubbing harder, I made sure to erase every ounce of blood from me. Once my skin was red and raw, I felt better, knowing that nothing of him remained on me.

I'd need to burn my clothes and scrub down my car just to be sure. It was the last bit of evidence tying me to the crime.

Washing my hair was significantly easier, the smell of Simon's products enough to keep my focus as I lathered and rinsed. When I climbed out, I spotted my bag, sending a silent thanks to Lennox for bringing it in.

Dressing into something clean and soft helped put the rest of my body at ease as I retraced the steps I'd taken to get here.

I'd been careful, avoided all cameras and took the back roads. I had to trust I was safe for now.

Brushing my wet hair in the mirror, I assessed myself. My face was blank, all emotion drained away from me. My eyes were dark, the spark having been stolen. I didn't like being this girl. I didn't want to go back.

Taking a deep breath, I forced myself to embrace my emotions, knowing if I ran from them this time, I'd never come back.

When I was satisfied with what I saw in the mirror, I gathered my stuff, careful not to touch any of the blood on the clothes.

Lennox was waiting for me outside the door when I exited.

"Hey, how do you feel?" she asked. Her eyes washed

over me, taking me in, almost like she was verifying I really wasn't hurt.

"Better. Is there somewhere I can burn these?" I asked, lifting the pile of things I'd been wearing.

Her eyes dropped to the wad of clothes, her head nodding before she looked up. "I know the perfect place."

She led me out back, tugging my hand as she stepped off the porch into a big backyard. Motion-sensor lights flashed on as we walked toward a brick circle a few yards from the house. When we neared, I realized it was a firepit.

"This work?" she asked, stopping to look at me.

"Yep." Tossing the clothes into the circle, I looked around for something to light them with.

"Here," Thane said from behind. I jumped a little but took the lighter fuel and matches he offered.

Squeezing some over the clothes, I stepped back as I thought about my next move.

"Here's to never looking back," I said, striking a match and tossing it into the pit.

Flames flew up, warming my cheeks, and I knew I meant that creed with everything in me.

Diary #1

Dear Mom,

A lot of crazy shit has happened since we last spoke. I don't want to get into it all, mostly because I don't want to relive it yet, but I know things will be different from here on out.

I'm at my friend Lennox's house, and I realized something tonight.

One, she's an amazing friend, willing to help me even if it puts her at risk.

Two, I want what she has. I'm a little envious of the easy way she can love the people in her life without fear of it being taken away.

I'd never begrudge her for having it. I know she fought for her life and for the love she has.

Which reminded me that I could do that too. I can fight.

So, I will stay with this man they seem to

believe will help me. And I'm going to protect myself. I'm never going to let another man try to take anything from me. Whether it be sex, my life, or my future, it's not going to happen anymore.

Are you ready to meet the new Darcie, Mom?

Love,

Me

CHAPTER 2

Darcie

LENNOX WOKE me entirely too early for my liking, and I was reconsidering our friendship until she placed a warm mug of coffee in my hands as I stumbled into the kitchen, my eyes half-closed.

"I can hear you grumbling. I thought you were a morning person?" she asked, sitting next to me at the bar.

Ignoring her for a second, I took a sip of the coffee, letting it fall over my tongue. The bitterness helped to ground me; the aroma aided in not wanting to roll back into bed, consequences be damned.

"You've only seen me after a pot of this stuff. Anyone can be a morning person after a pot of coffee," I finally said, opening my eyes to stare at her. "Besides, I don't think this counts as morning. This is sleepy time," I whined when I noticed the clock said it was 5 am.

"We're heading out at seven, so I wanted to ensure we had enough time to take care of you before we left."

I caught a hint of sadness wrapped around her words, making me wake up more. Finishing the last of the mug, I set it down on the counter before wrapping my arms around her. Lennox came easily to me, hugging me back just as fiercely.

"I wish we had more time. I hate that I have to leave. Just say the word, and I'll stay, Darce."

I pulled back, shaking my head. There wasn't any situation where I'd make her delay her dreams to save me. It just wasn't who I was.

"So, when do we talk to Bubba?" I asked, hoping to show her I was on board.

"We need to leave in twenty minutes," Slade said, walking into the kitchen wearing all black. His tattoos peaked out on his neck and hands, but everywhere else was covered. If you didn't know him, Slade painted a menacing picture. "I've moved your car to the barn. It will be safe there."

"Why can't I take it?" I asked, not liking that I'd be without a vehicle.

"I'm not saying you can't, just that I wouldn't. I know someone you can trade it with for a new one just in case you were captured on any CCTV footage or traffic cams you weren't aware of."

Sighing, I thought over his words, hearing the truth there. "Yeah, okay. I'll go change."

Sliding off the stool, Lennox squeezed my arm as I passed by. I offered her a sliver of a smile, my thoughts jumbled as I headed toward the room I was staying in.

I quickly pulled on a jean skirt, a flannel shirt, and my cowboy boots. I brushed my hair back, parting it into two pigtails before placing my cowboy hat on. If I was going to play a part, I might as well dress like it.

Gathering my bags, I double-checked that the few things I held dear were with me. My mother's music box and the contents of the safety deposit box were all in my bag with the journal. I instantly felt better knowing they were with me. I'd need to face the contents of the box one day, but I knew it wasn't this one.

Soon though.

I carried my two bags out toward the door, finding the rest of my belongings being loaded into the back of a van.

"This what you took on your road trip?" I asked, pointing toward the van.

"Yep. It was perfect," Lennox said, beaming a megawatt smile at me.

"You didn't, you know?" I asked, wiggling my eyebrows.

"What?" she asked, looking from me toward the van.

Simon snickered as he shut the back, clearly understanding my question. "It's safe from any bodily fluids, Darcie. We do have some restraint, you know."

Lennox's face turned red for a second then she shrugged, accepting that my question was valid when she had three boyfriends.

"Oh, I'm sure you do," I joked, deciding to pick at her some more. "It's Lennox I worry about."

She stuck her tongue out at me, twirling in her dress as it spun out around her, her colorful hair shining in the rising sun.

"Just you wait, Darce. I'll get you back one day."

"Bring it, short stuff."

"Short stuff! You're just as short," she hollered.

"Nah. I'm definitely an inch taller," I argued, enjoying the banter. I'd forgotten how much fun we had together.

Lennox rolled her eyes this time, huffing as she placed her hands on her hips. "I was going to be nice and tell you all about Bubba, but I think I'll keep it to myself."

"I already met the guy," I said, moving closer to the van. "I'm still unsure how he will protect me, but I'll give him a shot."

Lennox looked between Simon and Slade, her mouth opening like she wanted to say anything. I caught Simon shaking his head slightly, her mouth closing in response.

"Hmm, well, you'll see. Then we'll see who's teasing who!"

I wrapped my arm around her shoulders. "I've missed you, friend."

She tilted her head, knocking it into mine. "I've missed you too. You sure you don't want to come on tour?"

"Nope!" I practically shouted, stepping away as she chased me.

"Let's go," Slade said, stopping our fun as he slid into

the driver's seat. Simon took the passenger seat, leaving Lennox and me in the back.

"Where's Thane?" I asked, buckling in.

"He's finishing up some paperwork and getting the last few things we needed in town," Lennox answered. "By the way, if you want a way to make some money, we could use your help at the shop."

"The shop?" I asked, not understanding.

"Tattooed Hearts. Bubba's the manager of it now since we've been gone. But they never filled my front desk role, so you could help out there if you wanted. Slade said he'd tell Bubba to pay you in cash so you wouldn't have to worry about being tracked and all that."

I gulped, her generosity was more than I expected. "Thanks." I licked my lips, looking at the others and nodding that I appreciated the offer. "I might take you up on that. Mostly because I'm worried I'll get bored more than anything. I've been working every day that I can remember since I was a teen. I'm not a woman of leisure." I chuckled.

Lennox laughed as well, pleased I was going to give the shop a try. "You know, he's single, right?" she asked, lifting her eyebrows.

Rolling my eyes, I scoffed. "I highly doubt that a girl on the run is his type. I've had enough man problems to last me a lifetime."

"He's got two roommates that are attractive as well," she whispered.

"You sure this is for my safety? If Slade hadn't

suggested it first, I'd wonder if this was your way of setting me up."

Lennox giggled but dropped it, zipping her lips closed. I glanced out the window at the world beginning to wake up around us. I'd only been up here a few times, but I always forgot how beautiful Kentucky could be. There were hills and fields of crops, pastures full of animals, and a sky so clear that you got the true meaning of what country living was.

We pulled into a subdivision ten minutes later, Slade maneuvering the van around the curvy roads until we reached the end. He pulled into a cul-de-sac, heading toward the middle house. Several cars were parked around the circle, and a few bikes were sitting in the driveway under a carport.

The house was red-brick, one story with a few bushes lining the front. While the grass had seen better days, overall it wasn't a bad-looking house. Unsurprisingly, the neighborhood was quiet at the early hour, and I realized how strategic that move had been as well—limiting the number of eyes that saw Lennox and me together.

I had to give it to Slade. The man cared about my bestie a hell of a lot. It made me trust him a little more, knowing he wouldn't do anything to make her mad.

Lennox pulled open the door the second the van turned off, bounding toward the front door. I looked at the two guys, wondering if I should follow or stay here.

"Um, should I go?" I asked, some hesitation edging in my voice.

"Give her a minute," Simon said. Slade grunted in response, stepping out of the van and walking to her.

When the door opened, the man I'd met once at a party stood in the open space. He was shirtless, his barrel chest on display, covered in tattoos and ginger hair. Outside his beard, there wasn't any other hair on his head. The man was built like a tank, and the more I stared, the more I realized he was a ginger Vin Diesel with a Viking beard.

Shit. Did I suddenly have a thing for Bubba? No. I couldn't. He was at least ten years older than me, perhaps more. Besides, what I'd said to Lennox was true. I didn't need any more male drama. It had only brought me trouble my whole life.

Dropping my eyes to Lennox, I watched as she explained my situation. I wasn't sure what she was saying, but when his eyes glanced toward the van, I felt the immediate need to hide. Blue eyes seared into me, making my skin heat.

I was so focused on this that I missed the next few seconds as he dropped his blue orbs back to Lennox. He must've agreed because Lennox was bouncing on her toes, wrapping her arms around his neck, much to Slade's annoyance.

Lennox ran back to the van, a smile on her face as she neared. I flicked my gaze back toward Bubba and Slade, finding Slade shaking his hand and slapping him on the back. The door opened, jolting me out of my snooping, and I slid out of my seat, my cowboy boots hitting the pavement.

It felt like I was wading underwater as I picked up my bags and moved toward the front door. While I'd agreed to this, it felt odd to be going through with it now. Slade moved past me, probably heading to grab the few boxes I had. Lennox was talking a mile a minute in my ear as we approached, but I didn't hear a single word.

My eyes were fixed on the man in front of me. He was an unmovable force as he stood in his doorway, his thick arms crossed as he watched me approach.

"Bubba, in case you forgot, this is my bestie, Darcie. Thanks so much for doing this again. You're the absolute best, Bubba bear."

The man stayed stoic, his usual jovial smile long gone from his face. I didn't know if it was a good sign or not. He seemed more menacing this way, making me believe he could protect me. But it was odd to not see the laughing man I'd met before.

"Hi," I said, my voice almost cracking at the end. "Thanks for letting me stay."

"No problem." Bubba didn't say anything else but moved aside so we could enter.

Stepping into the house, I was surprised to find how tidy it was. If three grown men lived here, I expected it to be cluttered at the least.

Instead, I found a cozy home that was organized and clean. Boots were lined up against the wall, and hats and coats were on pegs. As we turned the corner, couches filled one space with a bookcase along one wall and a giant TV on another. A soft rug lay in the middle, pulling colors from the pillows and wall. It was tastefully decorated, making me more curious about these men.

A dining room was off to the left, a table that would seat about eight sitting in the center. A breakfast bar led to an open kitchen where I could make out a package of eggs and bread on the counter. It seemed we'd interrupted him preparing breakfast.

Dark hallways jetted off in either direction from the kitchen, stopping my perusal of the space. Slade and Simon entered with my boxes and placed them on the floor near my feet.

"Lennox, you got ten minutes," Slade said, nodding his goodbyes as he pushed Simon out the door.

Lennox hugged Bubba once more, whispering something in his ear before turning toward me. She grabbed my arm and walked to the door.

"Call me or text me whenever you can get a phone. I want to know you're okay. If you don't feel comfortable here, we can figure out another plan. My dad would help you, Darce."

She stopped, holding my hands in hers as she stared at me. I nodded to appease her, knowing going to her father was the last option I'd consider. He might be able to argue self-defense, but I didn't want to chance it. I was too pretty for prison.

"I promise. Go win America's heart. They're going to

love you, Len." I pulled her close, needing one more of her hugs to hold me until I could do it again.

She pulled back, wiping a tear, her smile a bit wobbly. "Be kind to him. He's the sweetest." She kissed my cheek and headed out the door.

The sound of it latching seemed to echo around me, and I knew I could only wait in this hallway for so long before it became weird.

Taking a deep breath, I headed toward the kitchen to find my new roommate.

Diary #2

Dear Mom,

I'm about to head to my new safe house with a man I've met once in passing. Lennox swears he's the one person I can trust. I trust her, so I'll give it a go.

I'm not sure what I'm really going to do here. When I left last night, I just needed to get away from it all, and this was the first place that came to mind.

Being only an hour from Nashville, I'm not exactly out of harm's reach. But I think it will work for now. I need to figure out a plan to get in touch with Maddox and see if his sister is alright. I need to talk to Dad too, but I doubt he'll respond. He hasn't in all these years.

I'm not really sure what my plan is beyond

that. I can't go back to Nashville or that life. So, I'll focus on this and figure the rest out later.

I wish you were here to give me advice, but I guess this is all I have. So, it will have to do.

As always, thanks for listening.

Love,

Me

CHAPTER 3

Bubba

I PUSHED the eggs around in the pan and flipped the bacon, trying to focus on what I was doing instead of where my mind wanted to go. It wasn't working, though, as I waited for the most gorgeous woman I'd ever seen to enter the kitchen.

Darcie was everything I wanted in a woman and someone I could never have. She was almost twenty years younger than me to start. It didn't help that she was Lennox's best friend and placed in my care to protect. I'd never forsake their trust like that by crossing a line.

No, Darcie would have to stay in my dreams where she'd been ever since I'd first laid eyes on her.

"What's cooking, good looking?" she sang as she entered the kitchen.

Her voice jolted me, causing me to splash bacon grease on my hand. Cursing, I jumped back and moved to the sink to rinse it.

"Shit. You okay?" she asked, moving toward me at the sink.

The smell of sunshine engulfed me, and I stopped breathing, not wanting it to leave my nostrils. Her hand touched mine, and I remembered I needed to let the air out in order to let more in.

"It's fine," I grunted and pulled my hand away.

I hadn't planned to sound so mean, but her touch hurt worse than the burn. It made me want her to touch me all over, something I couldn't entertain, or the part of me that didn't care about any of my reservations would make itself known.

"Anything I can do to help?" she asked, appearing to ignore my gruffness.

I counted to ten in my head, holding my hand to my chest as I moved back to the stove. I didn't ever want this woman to have to do anything again, but if it helped get her out of my presence for a few seconds, then it would be worth it.

"Plates are in that cabinet." I nodded toward the one on the left as I picked up the spatula. The eggs were over-done, and most of the bacon was burned, but it would have to suffice.

She hummed a song as she waltzed her cowboy boots over to the cabinet. I watched her out of the side of my eyes as she reached up and then stopped.

"How many?" she asked, turning toward me.

"Three. Brooks isn't here at the moment."

She pulled down three, then opened drawers until

she found the silverware. I could've told her, but watching her was more fun. She grabbed a few paper towels off the roll before walking to the breakfast bar and placing them down. It was sweet in a way I hadn't been prepared for.

"Drinks?" she asked, looking up at me when she was done.

"Coffee in the pot and juice in the fridge."

"Oh, you're my hero for the day. I need more coffee after Lennox woke me up at this forsaken hour."

A smile crept over my face, but I stopped it before she caught it. It would be better if she thought I barely tolerated her. It would help me keep my distance.

I grabbed the pan of eggs and dumped them onto the three plates, and followed with the bacon. I began scooping some off when I realized I'd given her as much as the other two plates.

"Don't you dare," she hissed. "I'm starved."

"You can eat all that?" I asked, looking at her directly. Which was a mistake I regretted immediately. Darcie's pale blue eyes stole my breath, and I had to remember how to breathe. Her round face looked up at me, a grin on her face. With her hair in pigtails and the cowboy hat on her head, I had difficulty remembering my name.

"Damn straight I can," she huffed, taking a seat at the bar.

I lifted my hands, leaving her to the food, knowing better than to come between a woman and her bacon.

"Sorry." I smiled, placing the pans in the sink.

"Pretty Boy!" I hollered, walking over and slapping the wall.

"I'm coming, grandpa!" he yelled back, stepping out of his room. His honey brown hair was messy as he rubbed his eyes, stubble covering his face. Thankfully, he wore pants since I'd forgotten to mention we had a guest.

I took the seat furthest from Darcie, leaving the one in the middle open. I didn't say anything, wanting to watch the show as Grayson spotted Darcie.

He stopped to grab a mug of coffee, filling it and taking a sip before he moved toward the bar. He was a few feet from it when he stopped, blinking.

"You're not Brooks," he mumbled.

"Nope," Darcie said, smiling. "What kind of name is Pretty Boy?" she asked, shoving a forkful of eggs into her mouth.

Grayson looked at me, searching my face for answers. I nodded, letting him know it was okay. He swallowed another gulp of coffee, his swagger waking up.

"Well, pretty lady, it's my road name. Do you know what that is?"

He leaned against the bar, giving her his best smile. When he wasn't working in the auto shop, he used that same smile to grace magazines and ads. It was why we'd given him the name "Pretty Boy" because he was too pretty to be a biker.

"A road name, huh?" Darcie stopped chewing, looking him up and down. I both hoped and dreaded what I knew would happen next. There wasn't a woman on the planet that could ignore Grayson's smile. "I take it you lost a bet then?"

A snort left my lips before I could stop it. I covered my mouth, hiding my smile as I smothered the rest of my laugh. Grayson's mouth hung open as Darcie giggled, eating her bacon like she hadn't stunned the man speechless.

"Better eat, *Pretty Boy*. You need to leave in twenty."

That broke the spell, and he moved around the bar, taking his seat between the two of us. "So, I guess my usual tactics won't work on you. How about we start over? I'm Grayson Lawson. People call me Grayson, Lawson, or Pretty Boy. You can take your pick. Now, do tell, who are you, and how long will you be here?"

I finished my plate and looked over, wondering what Darcie would share. Surprisingly, she was finishing her own, making me realize she hadn't been lying about her appetite. It made me like her more, which wasn't a good sign for how this was going to end.

"Hmm, I'll have to see which one fits you, I guess. For now, I'll stick with Grayson. I'm Darcie." She stuck out her hand, offering it to him. Grayson took it, bringing it to his lips to kiss.

"Pleasure's all mine, Darcie."

"Oh boy, you're a big flirt, aren't you?" She shook her head, smiling at him.

"We all have our talents," Grayson said, scooping the food into his mouth. "You didn't mention why you were here or how long."

"Ah, yes. You're more clever than I gave you credit for, then." She wiped her mouth and got up. Walking around Grayson, she motioned toward my plate, taking it when I nodded. She placed them both in the sink and turned on the water. Grayson looked at me, but I shook my head, leaving her to tell him what she wanted. Once she'd rinsed the plates and placed them in the drying rack, she turned, facing us both.

"Short version for now. I needed a place to lie low. Lennox suggested here since she was leaving town. And I promise to not wear out my welcome or interfere with whatever you have going on. I just need some time to figure out my next move."

"That sounds like there's a lot more of a story there," Grayson said, placing the last of the bacon in his mouth. Darcie moved forward and added his plate to the water she'd started.

"It's enough for now," I said, narrowing my eyes at him. He sighed but nodded. "Ten minutes."

Grayson took my warning and got up, heading to the bathroom. The shower turned on a few seconds later, and Darcie placed the other dishes onto the rack. I hadn't even realized she'd done the pans as well.

"You don't have to do that," I said, standing.

"I know. I wanted to. Thanks for breakfast." She dried her hands and turned toward me. "Lennox mentioned I could go to the shop with you and help out there."

I nodded, swallowing. I'd hoped she wouldn't want

to just yet. "Yeah. I'm heading out soon if you want to join me."

"If it's okay, I think I'll stay back today. I have some things I need to look into."

I sighed in relief, knowing I'd have a few hours out of her presence. "Yes, of course. Here, I'll show you the spare room." I picked up the boxes and walked down the hallway opposite where Grayson went. There were two spare rooms in the house, but I was putting her in the one the furthest away from me.

I opened the door and stepped in, setting the boxes on the bed. Some sunlight filtered through the windows, showcasing the dust that had been disturbed by my entrance. Darcie flipped the light switch when she entered, taking in the room.

It was a modest bedroom with a bed, desk, and closet. It had been another club member's a few years back, but it had stayed empty once he left.

"There's a bathroom across the hall. There should be towels in the closet. You'll share it with Brooks when he's back. Grayson and I are on the other end."

She nodded, taking in the space. "Thank you, Bubba."

"No problem. If you need anything, my number's on the fridge."

"Is there a place close by to get a phone?" she asked, turning toward me.

I rubbed the back of my head, wanting to give her everything and knowing I needed to keep some space.

"There are a few places in town, but nothing in walking distance. I'll take my bike in today and leave the keys for the truck if you want."

"You wouldn't mind me driving it?" she asked. Her eyelashes fluttered, and I wasn't sure if she was doing it on purpose.

"It sticks a little on second, but you should be good for the places you need to go. Assuming can you drive a stick," I asked, raising my eyebrow in challenge.

Her jaw ticked, and she took a deep breath, her eyes lighting up. "Better than you'll ever know."

I gulped, my tease had backfired big time on me and my face reddened. She winked, sitting on the bed and crossing her legs.

"I really do appreciate everything you're doing for me, Bubba."

"No problem. Lennox is like a little sister to me. If she says you need help, I'll do what I can."

"You know, you're different than I thought you'd be," she said, assessing me.

"How so?" I asked, despite telling myself not to.

"The way Lennox described you, I basically pictured you as an overgrown teddy bear. Like there wasn't anything menacing about you. I figured I'd be the one killing the spiders and whatnot."

Snorting for the second time in a matter of minutes, I couldn't stop the smile this time. Shaking my head, I gave her a look I knew I'd regret later, but nothing at that moment could stop me. I moved closer, towering over her until her back hit the wall. My hands braced against the wall, and I stared down at the blonde beauty.

"There's so much you don't know about me, little girl. If you're good, maybe you'll find out."

She sucked in a breath, her breasts heaving as she tried to slow her heart rate. Licking my lips, I forced myself to move away from the wall and out the door. I marched down the hall, debating if I had time to take a second shower, so I could get rid of the raging hard-on I now had.

In the end, I threw on some clothes, tossed the truck keys onto the counter with my cell phone number, and hopped onto my bike.

Grayson gave me a funny look as he climbed on his, but I shook my head, unable to talk. As the wind whipped around me on the way to the shop, I listed all the reasons why getting involved with Darcie was wrong.

The problem was that when I arrived at Tattooed Hearts, I couldn't remember why any of them were flaws.

This blonde bombshell was going to turn my world upside down. And something told me I was going to enjoy every minute of it.

Diary #3

Dear Mom,

Oh, man. I think I might have finally met my match. I'm not sure what it means yet, just that I'm a little shocked at the heat I felt between the big man and me.

The ginger has some fire.

Now that I've cooled off, I'm going to look around and head into town to get a few things I need. I'm going to start looking into Maddox and his sister today. If I have a plan, I'll feel better.

As much as I hate that I'm not with Lennox, the living situation is going well so far. I've met two of the guys. Slade was right about the fact their MC club wasn't what I was used to. The men here are kind and respectful. Nothing like the Diamonds, thank God.

Here's to hoping the last roommate isn't a total dickwad.
Until next time,
Your firecracker

CHAPTER 4

Darcie

BY THE TIME I'd scoped out the room and the rest of the house, it was already noon. I felt a little bad snooping through the guy's belongings, but if I was going to be staying here, I justified my need to be safe. Not that any of them had much stuff to peruse, but I learned a few things.

For instance, Grayson liked his hair care and moisturizer, with more bottles on his dresser than I'd ever owned. His room was clean, and everything had its place. I spent a few minutes switching out a couple of his drawers just to mess with him. I almost wished I could be there to see his face when he went to reach for his socks and found his jeans instead.

As his road name suggested, he was a pretty boy, making my toes curl just from a look. But something else about him made me want to keep talking to him, to find out more. Searching his room might have been unorthodox, but I felt safer around him now.

As for Bubba, there wasn't much to find in his room. He had a big bed with overstuffed pillows, a closet full of the same clothing, and a few pairs of boots at the bottom of the closet. There weren't any personal items on display. He had his own bathroom, which was as tidy and sparse as his room. His shower made me jealous, though, and I was already devising a plan to get him to allow me to use it.

The other room in their hallway was locked, along with Brooks'. I'd have to search through them later when I remembered how to pick a lock. It hadn't been part of the MCD program, but Maddox had shown me once. It was a vague memory, but with a refresher on YouTube, once I had a phone, I'd have those doors open in no time.

My stomach growling had me relenting in my search for the time being so I could head into town. Food and a phone were first on my list.

Sorting through my boxes, I changed into an oversized shirt and a pair of jeans. As much as I liked my cowgirl look, I didn't want to draw attention when I was alone. My room looked like a tornado had hit it, but I didn't have time to deal with it now. I'd unpack later once the monster in my belly was fed.

Baseball cap pulled down low, I pulled myself into the truck. It was so high I practically needed a stepladder. The truck was an older one, and I had to move the seat in order to reach the pedals. My pulse skyrocketed as I turned the engine over. Anxiety coursed through me at driving a stick, but I reminded myself that if I could drive a bike, I could also do this.

It wasn't my best lie, but it was all I had at the moment as I backed out of the drive.

The truck was smoother than I expected, only slightly sticking, as Bubba had said, in second. Once I was out of the subdivision, I headed into town, focusing on the road, my hands at ten and two.

A strip mall came into view within a few minutes, and I sighed in relief. My whole body vibrated when I parked in the lot, a million miles away from any other cars. I'd probably regret it later when I was returning to it, but not having anyone around to park next to felt safer.

Keeping my head low, I searched the stores, finding a pawnshop, a Chinese restaurant, a sandwich shop, a jewelry store, a beauty shop, and an electronics store on the end.

Heading to the electronics store first, I sighed in relief when it was a girl on the floor. I was hoping she'd be less likely to remember me and more sympathetic to my cause than a man.

She smiled as I neared, and I shoved my hands into my pockets to keep myself from fidgeting.

"How can I help ya?" she asked, smiling politely.

"I need to get a prepaid phone. Do you have those?" I asked, keeping my voice low.

"Sure do. One sec, I'll bring up the models."

She smiled again before she walked to the back of the store. It didn't take her long before she was returning with two plastic-encased phones. She went over the different features, but I stopped her, already knowing which one I wanted.

"This one will be perfect. Do you have any resell tablets as well?"

"Sorry, hun. We don't carry anything like that. You might try the pawnshop on the other end. They tend to have a few."

I paid for the phone, thanking her for the help. My stomach rumbled again, so I walked to the Chinese restaurant, deciding to order and then pop into the pawnshop while my food was being made.

"This all for you?" the lady asked, eyeing me up and down after I ordered four meals.

"Yup. I want to try it all," I said, giving her a grin as I nodded.

She chuckled, giving me a big smile. "Alright, I'll throw in some chow mein, too. You'll like it. Be twenty minutes."

"Perfect. I'm going to pop over to the pawnshop. I'll be right back."

Her face tightened, and she nodded, her eyes narrowing a little. "Be quick," she said, and I wondered if she wanted to say more but wasn't sure how. It didn't sound like she was saying to hurry so she wouldn't be waiting on me; more like she didn't want me in there long.

Taking her words at face value, I nodded and headed to the shop; my mission to find a tablet and get out was playing on repeat in my head.

Stepping into the crowded space, I instantly felt eyes on me. It was probably a familiar feeling in a place like this where they watched everyone like a hawk, afraid they might steal something. When I came around a stack of fax machines and old computer parts, I found the clerk leaning against the counter, his eyes fixed on me.

"You looking for anything, sweetheart?" he asked. He had a toothpick in the corner of his mouth, which he pulled out to lick his lips before placing it back in.

Holding in my disgust, I walked forward a little. "I'm looking for a tablet. Do you have anything?"

He pointed with that same toothpick to a corner in the back. Smiling tightly, I headed there, keeping him in my peripheral. I suddenly understood the woman next door's meaning. This guy was a creep.

The section he pointed me to had several tablets. I looked them over, going for one of the cheaper ones that turned on and wasn't too scratched up. I only needed it for simple things, so I didn't need to blow all my cash. Picking up the charger that went with it, I headed to the front, wanting to get out of there. His eyes had stayed on me the entire time, and they no longer felt like they were watching for me to steal but more predatory.

"I'll take this," I said, laying it down.

"Hmph, fill out this card here in case I need to get in

touch." He slid across a piece of paper before taking the items and punching in a total on the register.

There was no way I was giving him any factual information, so I made up a name and used the street number from my old house in Mississippi with a Tennessee zip code. It should look legit enough for him, but it wouldn't have any trail to me afterward.

I glanced at the total, seeing he'd added a charge.

"What's that for?" I asked. The prospect of paying it felt wrong, but if it got me out of here quicker, I might be obliged.

"Processing charge," he said, smiling with his toothpick. "There's another way to take care of it if you're interested."

Chills ran down my spine, and I decided to deal with the extra fifty and get out of there. Grimacing, I shook my head, pulling out the exact change and placing it on the counter with the info card. I reached for the tablet when his hand smacked down on top of mine, jolting me. Gasping, I glanced up, finding his predatory smile directed at me.

"You sure you don't want to make arrangements? Maybe I should add another charge," he purred, his eyes scanning down my body. Despite knowing I was fully covered, it felt like he was undressing me, violating me in a way I hadn't felt since the night Agonizer raped me.

My body froze, the memories of that night filtered through as I tried to grasp onto reality and determine how to get out of this situation. I couldn't fight him. I didn't need the attention, nor did I want to run again after just getting here. No, this required a delicate solution.

The door pinged as it opened, breaking whatever trance he'd frozen me in. The woman next door peered in, holding up the food bags.

"Your order's ready," she yelled, not looking at the man.

He glared at her, but it allowed me to grab the tablet and bolt out the door. My heart was racing, but with each step closer to the door, the better I felt.

She opened the door wider as I neared, not saying anything until we were both free.

"Thank you," I said, my hands shaking as I tried to get myself together.

"Be safe, child. My son will walk you to your car."

A man I hadn't noticed stood behind her, taking the bags of food. Tears pricked my eyes at the realization they were watching out for me.

"Thank you. I can't..." I started, my throat closing up at the genuine warmth I felt for this stranger.

She patted my hand, urging me to go. Nodding, I thanked her once again before heading toward the truck. I felt terrible that her son had to walk all the way, regretting parking so far away. But I was glad to have him since I'd noticed the pawn shop owner move toward the door, watching.

The boy nodded as I thanked him, climbing into the truck a few minutes later. It took me another five before my hands were no longer shaking and I was calm enough to start the engine.

"Fiddlesticks!" I shouted, hitting the steering wheel in frustration. I had to be more careful moving forward. I couldn't always count on the kindness of others to save me. I was one wrong move away from ending up in jail or as someone's 'well guest' so they could wear me as a skin suit. I didn't have it in me to put the lotion in the basket.

Neither option was how I wanted to spend my life.

"Get back, eat some food, and find Maddox," I whispered, needing a plan. "Freak-out later."

Nodding, I turned the keys and shifted the truck, making sure to go in the other direction so I could avoid the pawn shop altogether.

It took me a few missed turns, but I finally returned to Bubba's house. Feeling better about my adventure and what I'd accomplished, I brought in my food and sat it on the counter. After peeking in a few cabinets, I found a plate and a fork. Dishing out a small portion of each, I devoured the food as I set up my new devices.

The phone was easy since I wasn't putting any contacts in it outside of a few people. I texted Lennox, letting her know it was my number and added Bubba's.

The brat part of me wanted to text him something to push his buttons, but the mature part knew it would only reinforce what he believed about me—that I was a spoiled princess, incapable of taking care of herself.

It bothered me that he thought I was weak and too young for him. Despite already deciding I wouldn't like him; I wanted that decision to be mine, and it felt like he'd already made up his mind before he even knew me.

The fire within wanted to punish him, while the reasonable part of me knew it wouldn't work out as I'd hoped. For now, I needed to show I wasn't a burden like a child he had to watch.

Cleaning up my mess, I put the rest of the food into the fridge and left a note that they could have whatever they wanted. It felt like the nice thing to do since they were letting me stay here.

Taking my devices with me to my room, I organized my things into neater piles so they'd be easier to find when I needed them. I didn't want to unpack completely in case I needed to make a run for it again. I could always send for the things at least if I needed them once I was settled.

Plopping down on the bed, I signed onto the server to see if there was any sign of Maddox. As it loaded, my eyes grew heavy, and I placed it down next to me, promising to only close my eyes for a few minutes.

Diary #4

Dear Maddox,

It feels strange writing to you this way, but since I can't seem to get a hold of you any other way, I thought I'd give it a try.

Despite everything that has transpired between us, you're still one of the few people I trust. I'll probably always love you, even if I never see you again.

I recently saw Chase for who he was. You were right; he wasn't to be trusted. I'm sorry it took me so long to figure that out.

He told me some things that were upsetting. About me, about you, about your sister.

I'm going to do what I can to find the truth. Too many years have passed at this point to not do something. I'm tired of the lies, and if anything, at least I'll finally know.

I hate the thought of you in jail, but it also gives me a sense of peace. I hate that it does. I'm sorry.

I'm hoping to find out some info soon, and when I do, be prepared to be rescued all hero style. It's my new thing.

I miss you, Maddox.

I still think Mad Dog is a stupid name.

Love,

Your Rosebud

CHAPTER 5

Maddox

THE METAL BARS CLANGED, the only warning before they opened into our cell block echoed in my ears. It was a familiar sound, one I'd grown used to over the past two years. With each day being the same, time felt slow, with hardly anything new to mark them by.

So, when the guard alerted me that I had a visitor, I stumbled, not expecting it.

"King, did you hear me?" he asked, looking at me strangely.

"Yeah. Sorry." I blinked, setting down the mop I'd been using, and placed it back on my cart. I nodded to the other guard, letting him know I was done. He walked over to inspect it as I walked out, following the guard who'd come to retrieve me.

"Do you know who it is?" I asked once we were clear of the other prisoners.

It had been hard at first coming in here. There hadn't been a lot of friendly faces, considering who I was; my father was not very popular in this neck of the woods. It took time for me to gain the trust of a few inmates and guards, showing them I wasn't like my father.

There were a lot of tests and punishments until I'd proven I wasn't joining sides. Once it was known I was a free man, things calmed down, and I didn't have to sleep with a shiv in my hand.

Those first few months had been rough; some of them had left me wondering if I'd make it. Only the thoughts of my sister and Darcie kept me going. They both needed me, and if I was honest, I needed them. They reminded me I was more than the thug my father wanted me to be. Instead, I was the man Tank had helped me become.

The guard looked at me, shaking his head. McDaniels was fair and strove to do his job well, not taking bribes and helping the men to be better than they'd entered. He was one of the good ones.

"Someone in a suit. I didn't get a name before I was sent to retrieve you. Do you think it's them?"

I stopped, needing a second to think. McDaniels stopped a few feet ahead, waiting for me to run the facts through my head. When I felt prepared, I began walking and caught up with him.

"Maybe. Once I could use the internet, I sent a secure message to the Mavericks, hoping Tank's allies could help me. It's been so long that I'd given up hope they could."

A smile spread as hope bloomed in my chest. This could finally be the moment I'd been waiting for.

The charges against me had been bogus, but with planted witnesses, it had been an open-and-shut case. I'd been told to take the plea deal to lessen my sentence, as no jury around here would ever find me not guilty.

I hated it, but I could understand the court-appointed attorney's position. Besides, it was what my father wanted. And what he desired, he got. If I didn't go to jail to serve some bogus charge, he'd make it so I was buried six feet under.

Whatever he'd traded for my freedom had been bad enough for him to want to undermine me the way he did. That, or he'd finally figured out my plan all along. I wasn't sure the Destroyer was that intuitive, but I'd learned from an early age to never underestimate him. Just when you thought you were safe, he would strike, reminding you why he was named the Destroyer.

McDaniels patted me on the back as we neared the visiting room, nodding to the guard at the door to let me through. I blanked my face, the mask I'd worn for so long feeling comfortable as I stepped into the room, eyeing the man at the table.

He was dressed in a nice gray suit, one that had to be expensive. Immediately, I knew he wasn't from the court. Could he be the ally finally coming to meet? Or was this something else?

The man watched me as I entered, waving away the guard as I took a seat. Whoever he was, he was comfortable enough in himself to not fear me. I didn't know if that was a good thing or not. It spoke of the power this man could wield, but what would that mean for me?

"Who are you?" I asked when he didn't say anything, his eyes assessing me behind wire-rimmed glasses.

"The better question," he said, "is what can I do for you?"

"Fine." I rolled my eyes, leaning back in my chair and crossing my thick arms across my chest. My tattoos peeked out as I tried to regain some of the power dynamic between us. "What can *you* do for me?" I asked through gritted teeth.

He smiled, practically giddy, as he watched me. "Oh, you're perfect."

Smacking my hands down on the metal table, I smiled in glee when he jumped a little. "Tell me why you're here, or I'll show you what my fists can do," I threatened. I had no intention of punching the man, but his demeanor was getting on my nerves.

He sighed like I was boring him, taking out a handkerchief to wipe his glasses. My jaw ticked as I waited, the anxiety coursing through me the longer he took. I had no more moves left, and he knew it.

Once he was finished, he placed his glasses back on his face and delicately folded the cloth. When it was folded back into the perfect square, he put it in his suit pocket, a little tuft sticking up. My face was red by this point, and I could imagine steam was about to roll out of my ears.

Pushing off the table, the chair screeched out behind me; the sound hurting my ears in the quiet space. I ignored it as I stood and began walking toward the door.

"I can get you out of here, Mr. King. Now, sit down and drop the macho act so we can get down to business. We only have a short amount of time to cover everything."

Gritting my teeth, my jaw flexed as I debated giving this guy any more of my time. Deciding I had nothing to lose by hearing him out other than missing a few hours of mopping, I sat down.

He opened a file folder, turning it toward me.

"I believe you know this man fairly well?" he asked, showing me a picture of none other than the Destroyer.

"Is that a trick question?" I asked, trying to gauge what his game was. "It's my father, but you already knew that."

He smiled, the movement feeling a bit too perfect. "Yes, you are correct. And if I was to believe what I've heard, you're not a fan of him. In fact, he's the reason you're in here? He set you up to take the fall for him when the Feds were getting too close."

I grunted, not wanting to say too much. It was a battle of wills to determine who had the true upper hand here.

"A colleague of mine sent me your name and file, telling me that you just might be the person I've been looking for."

"Sorry to break it to you, but you're not my type.

Besides, I'm taken." I raised my eyebrows at him, daring him to continue.

He chuckled, not flummoxed at all by my comment. "Ah, there's that wit Hank spoke of."

The mentioning of Darcie's father had me sitting up straighter. "You know Hank?" I asked, trying to keep the relief out of my voice.

"We have a mutual friend."

"So what is it you're wanting from me?" I asked, knowing this game all too well. He wouldn't help me unless I could give him something—or someone.

"Smart too. I bet your fellow inmates resent you for that." He joked, pointing toward the cell block. "Well, you see, Mr. King, I have a personal reason for wanting a man behind bars. The reason doesn't matter per se, just whether or not you're willing to help. In the process, we might be able to get you out of here and put two men away."

"Who?" I asked, excitement building low in my stomach. It felt too good to be true, so I wanted to hedge it carefully so I didn't come out on the losing end.

"Stanley Driscoll and your father."

The air left the room at the mention of those two men. Putting my father away alone was enough to make me break out in a sweat. If he was ever released or found a loophole to avoid jail time, I'd be a dead man. The same could be said for the Agonizer. Both men were killers, willing to do literally anything to stay out from behind bars.

I swallowed, my hands beginning to shake under the table. Sweat dripped down my back as I thought over his words.

"What are you offering, and what would I have to do?"

He smiled smugly like he believed he already had me. But I knew the danger and the risks. I could be out in a year on parole for good behavior if I kept things going as they were. It would be hard to leverage that for something full of risk.

"You give me Stanley Driscoll, then all the charges against you will be dropped, and your record will be expunged. If you take out your father in the same wave, we'll set you up with a new identity."

"That's a lot for me to risk. Neither of those men will be easy to charge. I know how this game works. They'll get someone lower on the ladder," I pointed at myself, "to take the fall. Nothing ever sticks to them. You're asking me to walk into my own murder."

He watched me again, that calculating look on his face. "You are clever. Fine, we'll ensure no fallback comes on you. If you fail, you'll return and finish your sentence in a cushy white-collar prison. Without any time added. It will be like you never left. How does that sound?"

It was the best offer I could hope for, but something about it still felt off. He was willing to give me a clean slate for turning over two of the deadliest men in the country. It wouldn't be easy, but it could mean I'd be back in Darcie's life quicker with all my baggage forgotten.

There might be a trap somewhere, but if the worst-case scenario meant I could return to a better prison to finish my sentence, there wasn't anything else they could do to me. It was the safety net I needed.

"What do I have to do?"

His clinical smile returned as he went over the things they knew and what they'd want from me. I was able to fill in some of the gaps from my time with both men. But there was still a lot I needed.

"I'll have the papers ready for you to sign tomorrow," he said, putting his file back in his briefcase.

"We start with my father first. Otherwise, there's no way I'll make it out of the state."

"Agreed. We only need a few more items to take him down. Your assistance will increase our odds of making it happen. It's been nice working with you, Mr. King."

He shook my hand, and I realized I still didn't know his name.

"You never did tell me who you were?" I hedged, hoping to finally know the man I was dealing with.

"It's better that you don't know. For our purposes, you can call me Agent Bones." He smiled like he'd just told the punchline of a joke no one else knew.

McDaniels was waiting for me when I stepped out, walking with me back to my cell. He asked me if he was the ally I'd thought, but I shook my head, not sure what to call Agent Bones.

I didn't feel like he was against me at the moment, but with a man like him, it felt like that could change quickly if I stepped out of line. So, no, he wasn't an ally. But he wasn't exactly an enemy, either. At least not yet.

For now, I'd call him Agent Bones and pray that I hadn't just signed my own death certificate.

Diary #5

Dear Dad,

I thought about you today. I was driving this manual truck, and it brought back memories of you teaching me how to drive. You were a terrible teacher, by the way, when it came to four-wheeled vehicles. I still have to count my blessings each time I make it anywhere safely.

I was born to ride. That's not something I can change just because I'm no longer part of the Mavericks.

For a long time, I was furious at you. I understood what you did but not why you cut me out of your life. Especially when I saw you still talked with Maddox. Why wasn't I special enough to check in on?

But I think I get it now. It hurts. It hurts to wait around for a letter or words from someone to know how they're doing. Perhaps a clean break was easier. I don't know. I haven't managed to do that yet.

Maybe I'm stronger than you in that sense. I can't seem to let Maddox go, no matter how long it's been or how much it hurts.

He's a part of me, and I'm part of him.

But I miss you. So, maybe if I write to you this way, I can finally resolve all the feelings I've been carrying around with me, and one day, I can forgive you.

That day is not today.

Your Daughter

VOICES TRICKLED into my open door, stirring me out of my stupor. I opened my eyes, rubbing them as I sat up. Drool was crusted on my chin, so I wiped it, licking my lips to wet them.

I'd fallen asleep and slept hard. The room was pitch dark, with only a tiny tendril of light coming through the windows. I glanced at the phone I'd just gotten to note the time—7 pm.

Damn. I'd been out for a good four hours.

Picking up the tablet, the red icon of the battery flashed telling me it was dead. So I got off the bed and plugged it in, setting it on the dresser. I was still wearing the baggy shirt from earlier, my hair a mess in the pony-tail I'd pulled it back into. While I didn't want to seem like a diva and change now that they were home, I had an odd desire to push buttons where these two men were concerned.

Pulling out a pair of yoga pants, I replaced the jeans and pulled on a crop top and a long cardigan. It was comfy, with a hint of sexuality. Running a brush through my hair, I made my way toward the noise.

I spotted a guy with his back to me first; his shaggy brown hair was longer than the other guys, covering his ears and down his neck. He wore a blue shirt and jeans, his legs spread as he told a story to Bubba, who was facing him. I could spot Grayson in the background near the stove.

Hesitating, I realized it must be the third roommate. I slowed my steps, not wanting to interrupt. When his voice hit my ears, I froze.

It was deep, smooth, and one I'd listened to countless nights.

But how could that be?

Frozen in my tracks, I blinked when Bubba spotted me, calling for me to enter the kitchen.

"Brooks, this is Darcie. Darcie, this is Brooks or Cowboy."

I smiled, taking in the face of the man I'd been intimate with, but had never seen. He had a strong jawline covered with stubble, sharp cheekbones, and green eyes that were so bright, I almost squinted. He was gorgeous, and I was staring right at him. His face turned red, some of the shyness I remembered coming to light.

"Howdy," he said, tilting his head toward me. His voice rolled over me, hitting all my spots like it used to. I opened my mouth to say something when Pretty Boy walked over, slinging his arm around me.

"How was your day, sugar?" he asked, smiling down at me.

"Um, fine," I whispered, clearing my throat. I suddenly had the urge to hide my identity in case I was wrong. If this was my Shy Cowboy, then I wanted that reunion in private.

I looked at Bubba, who was watching me, his eyes narrowed. "Truck do alright?"

I nodded, pulling my cardigan together. I no longer had the urge to push buttons.

"Thanks for the leftovers. I was starved when I got in and ate quite a bit," Brooks said, his voice softer. Did he recognize me?

I smiled, nodding as well. I wasn't one to ever be at a loss for words, but they no longer wanted to come to me.

"Well, I think I'm going to unpack," I whispered, heading to my room before they could question me. I walked quickly, shutting the door behind me and leaning against it.

This place just got a whole lot more interesting.

I SKIPPED DINNER, UNABLE TO FIND THE courage to sit through an entire meal and not speak. Everything in my boxes and bags was now organized as I sat on the bed, staring at them. It was odd how the contents of my life fit into this room.

A few personal items, a box I wasn't ready to open yet, and a week's worth of clothes. Since I'd packed them at random, I had an eclectic assortment. Along with my cowboy boots and hat, I also had a leather jacket and leather pants, a few dresses, some shorts, and flannels. The only other shoes I had that weren't boots were high heels and the old pair of sneakers I'd worn earlier.

I was going to need to remedy the wardrobe situation quickly, or I'd look like an extra from a country music video.

My stomach growled, and I winced. While my heart couldn't take sitting there without knowing, my stomach didn't agree. It was about ten o'clock now, so I listened, trying to hear all the sounds of the house. There was a TV on somewhere, but it was low, making me wonder if it was being watched or just on for noise.

A washer tumbled in the distance, but I couldn't hear anyone else moving. Taking a deep breath, I stepped out into the hall and looked both ways. It was clear, so I tiptoed down the hallway toward the kitchen.

If I had to eat Chinese again, I would. My stomach wholeheartedly agreed.

To my utter amazement, a plate covered in plastic wrap sat on the counter, a note sitting on top of it.

Darcie,

You better eat, or I'll sic Lennox on you.

We leave for the shop at 7 tomorrow morning. Inventory. If you're not out here, I'm leaving you.
-Bubba

I smiled, then stopped myself. While I wanted to push his buttons, under no circumstances was I to fall for the overbearing teddy bear. I wouldn't allow it.

Placing the plate into the microwave to heat, I grabbed a glass and filled it with water while I waited. Wonderful food smells filled the space, my taste buds rejoicing at the nearness of food. It wasn't long before it was ready, and I pulled it out, amazed at the food Grayson had made.

It looked like some kind of stir-fry with noodles, vegetables, and chicken. I immediately shoveled it into my mouth as the flavor exploded over my tongue.

"Okay, Grayson has some skills," I mumbled around the forkful.

I heard a chuckle behind me, but I didn't stop to see who it was. I was having a love affair with this plate at the moment.

"I'm glad you approve, pretty lady!"

Rolling my eyes at the name, I cleared my plate and turned to him. "While I don't love the nickname, I do have to give you credit for this meal. Thank you for saving me some. It was incredible. I had no idea you could cook."

He smirked, moving closer. It didn't go unnoticed that he was only in a pair of sweatpants and nothing else —gray sweatpants, at that.

I quickly brought my eyes back up, not wanting to fall into the thirst trap laid before me.

"There's a lot of things you don't know about, Darcie."

"Fair. I've only known you for about an hour."

"Want to get to know me more?" he asked, brushing my hair over my shoulder.

Tingles ran down my arm as goosebumps erupted. Everything in me wanted to say yes, but I knew I needed to slow play this, or we'd crash and burn before the weekend.

"Hmm, I'll pass. Thanks for the food."

I spun on my heels and rinsed my plate, biting my lip the entire time. I desperately wanted to turn around and see his expression, but it only worked if I pretended to be disinterested.

So, despite my yearning, I kept my back to him and walked out of the kitchen toward my room. I could've sworn I heard a chuckle, but it was too faint to know for sure.

With my stomach happy, I crawled into bed, hoping to find some peace.

SLEEP DID NOT COME. TAKING A FOUR-HOUR NAP in the middle of the day really screwed with one's sleep schedule.

Tossing and turning again, I pulled my phone off the nightstand to check the time, 11:30 pm. It had only been an hour since I'd returned to this room! Groaning, I sat up, knowing what I needed to do. I wouldn't be able to move forward until it was done.

Climbing out of my bed, I walked to the door and peered out again. The house was quieter, like everyone was asleep now. Taking a deep breath, I moved further down the hallway toward the room I hadn't been able to search yet.

My hands shook as I lifted them to knock. My knuckles grazed against the wood, barely making a sound. Taking another breath, I calmed myself before striking out a little harder this time.

The sound of someone stirring could be heard deeper into the room, so I stepped back to wait. Footsteps approached, and I sucked in a breath as anxiety exploded in my body.

Just do it and get it over with. Then you'll know.

I didn't have time to ponder my conversation with myself as the door opened, a blurry-eyed Cowboy standing before me.

He wore only a pair of boxers, leaving his body on display—a body I was very familiar with. I gasped, knowing unequivocally that it was him. *My Cowboy.*

The sound made him blink, his eyes opening wider.

When he realized it was me at the door, he pulled it more in front of him. I'd forgotten how shy he said he was with girls.

"Um, hi. Did you need something?" he asked, looking at me curiously.

I didn't think, unable to hold it in any longer. So I ripped the bandage off, diving in head-on.

"Cowboy, it's me. It's—"

"Rose?" he asked, his eyes wide.

He opened the door for a second, and I worried he was about to close it in my face when his arm reached out and pulled me into the dark room. His hands touched my shoulder lightly like he was afraid to do so.

"Is it really you, Rose? I thought...." He shook his head. "One sec. I can't talk with you while I'm practically naked." His hands dropped off my shoulders as he moved to grab something

"That's funny since it was usually the only way we did talk."

He chuckled but continued on his search for something. I heard him pulling a shirt over his head, and a second later, a small light turned on.

"Come here and sit. I have so many questions."

I did as he asked, sitting on the corner of his bed. He sat further up but reached out to grab my hand. He was hesitant and shy but seemed to push past it, desperate to touch me, to make sure I was real.

I understood because I felt the same.

"How? What happened? I... yeah, I don't know what

to ask." He chuckled, the sound so familiar to me that it warmed my insides.

"Each of those questions have different answers, so I guess I'll start with what happened. Do you remember Candie? The one who introduced me to the site?"

He nodded, his thumb running across my fingers.

"Well, she started seeing one of her clients in real life, and they found out. In the process, everyone was locked out. There were some minors or something too, and the site got the attention of the FBI. I was so mad at myself that I hadn't worked out another way to contact you. I hated that I didn't get to tell you or say goodbye. You were one of the best parts of the whole thing."

He smiled, and my heart jumped in my chest. It was odd putting the voice and body to his face now. It was like there were two beings, and I had to merge them together.

"I don't know what that says about me that I like hearing that."

"I think it just means we made a real connection. You always said you wished we could meet in real life... Well, here we are."

"Here we are," he said softly before his nose scrunched. "But how?"

I sighed, not sure how much I wanted to share. "Do you know Lennox?" I asked, figuring I could start there.

"Yeah. She works with Waylon."

"Who?" I asked, momentarily stunned.

"You know, big bald ginger down the hall?"

"Bubba?" I asked, a smile spreading across my face. Cowboy nodded.

"Yeah, that's his road name. Waylon's his real name. That's what I call him."

"I like it. I can't wait to call him that." I snickered, loving that I found another button.

Cowboy shook his head at me like I was too cute for words.

"And you're Brooks? You're still Shy Cowboy in my head."

His face tinted pink. "Yeah. Brooks Langston. Cowboy is my road name because of the rodeo."

"Brooks," I said, letting his name roll around on my tongue. "And the rodeo?"

"I'll tell you all about it later."

"Fair." I sighed, knowing I needed to explain. "Well, Lennox is my best friend. I got into trouble a few days ago and had to leave my place quickly. I needed somewhere to go until I could figure out what to do. So I came here. Unfortunately for me, but good for her, she was heading out on tour this morning. Slade suggested Bubba, and here I am."

His grip had become stronger at the mention of trouble, and he stared at me, knowing I wasn't telling everything.

"What kind of trouble?"

"The MC kind."

He swallowed, his eyes searching mine for something.

"What aren't you saying, Rose?"

I sighed, dropping my eyes to the blanket. I played with the fabric as I debated how much to share. This wasn't a random person. This was Cowboy. My Cowboy.

"Are you sure you want to know? Once you do, it's not something you can unlearn."

I peered up at him from beneath my eyelashes. His eyes were locked onto my face. They were strong and unmoving, offering me a strength I desperately needed.

"I just found you again, Rose. I'm not going to lose you over being scared. I want to know. I can handle it."

Taking his word for it, I started at the beginning with Maddox and the Mavericks. I told him about my dad, the Agonizer, and Chase. He pulled me into his arms at some point, and we rested against the headboard as I continued my tale of woe and heartbreak. I shared how I came to Nashville on my own, finding myself in the midst of everything and learning to trust. How he'd helped me with taking back my body and sexuality.

I didn't know how long I talked, just that I was spent by the end. Emotionally and mentally.

"There aren't words to describe how amazing I think you are, Darcie. You truly have bloomed into a beautiful rose. Thank you for honoring me with your story. Now, rest. Close your eyes and sleep. I got you."

I didn't fight it. What was the point? Snuggling down under the covers, I rested on his chest, his heartbeat comforting as I fell asleep in his arms.

Diary #6

Dear Mom,

I'm at a loss for words. Something good finally happened from this mess, and I know I don't want to screw it up.

I thought coming here would be torture, but the three guys have all been sweet so far. Well, Bubba is more gruff than sweet, but I think I'm wearing him down.

Pretty Boy is fun and makes me smile.

Bubba gives me someone to mess with.

And Cowboy... I'm just so happy to have my friend back.

I'm not sure what it means, but I'm really glad I'm here.

Love,

Darcie

CHAPTER 7

Darcie

THE FEELING of a body next to me had me bolting upright, my heart racing as I panicked. Where was I? Who was I with?

I searched for something familiar in the dark room but came up empty. My breathing became choppy as I tried to recall what had happened last night.

I glanced at the bare chest next to me and suddenly remembered.

Cowboy. I found my Shy Cowboy last night.

Placing my hand on my heart, I took deep breaths as I tried to regain some sense of calm. I vaguely remembered talking late into the night and snuggling down, confident I wouldn't fall asleep in here.

The fact I had was more shocking than anything.

Since Maddox, I hadn't slept next to anyone, let alone another man. Waking up to someone new was strange and not an activity I was used to. Did I get up before he did and pretend I wasn't here? Did I wake him up to let him know I was leaving? Would the others see me? What would that mean?

"Wake up call," a voice shouted, followed by banging on the door. "Your turn to make breakfast."

Brooks moved next to me, his eyes opening slowly as he woke. When he spotted me, his hand reached out, cupping my face.

"I thought I'd dreamed you, but here you are, more beautiful than I could've imagined."

His words melted me on the spot, and I leaned down, my eyes searching his. It was strange to know this man intimately in a way but not in others. The touch of his hand against my face was new. The way his green eyes shifted back and forth and the few freckles I could spot on his nose were too.

I was discovering who he was all over again.

"Good morning," I whispered, smiling at him. "I hope I didn't do anything embarrassing in my sleep."

He smiled, shaking his head, his chestnut waves moving against the pillow. "I don't think that's possible. What are you doing today?" he asked, sitting up and stretching.

My eyes trailed over his torso, matching the visions of his abs cemented in my head. My pulse raced for a different reason this time.

"I was going to help out at Tattooed Hearts."

He nodded, throwing the covers off and standing. As he stretched, I could watch him a little more, taking in all the dips and curves as I placed them on his tall frame.

My brain was still struggling with knowing parts of his body and realigning them with reality.

"Do you mind if I grab a shower first? It's my turn to make breakfast."

"No, go ahead. I need to head back to my room and get my stuff. Just knock on my door when you're done."

Brooks smiled, walking over and taking my hand. "I really want to kiss you. Hell, my body really wants to do more. You're a walking aphrodisiac to my cock." His face turned red, but he continued. "I want all those things and so much more, so I will wait and earn them the right way. I just wanted you to know that."

Warmth spread through me, his acknowledgment of his feelings and what he wanted from me, taking me by surprise.

"I want that too."

"Plus, I need to share something with you before any of that happens. Can we talk again tonight?"

"Yeah. You can come to my room this time," I teased, giving him a wink.

"It's a date."

Going up on my tiptoes, I kissed his cheek and headed to the door. I stopped, glancing back into the room when I got to the door, spotting him with his eyes closed, a hand to the spot I'd just kissed. It was enough to make my heart burst as I continued toward my room.

I thought coming here would be a temporary stopping ground, a place to reset and organize my next move. It had already turned out to be so much more than that, and I'd only been here two days.

Sorting through my clothing items, I picked out a dress that would work with my cowboy boots and grabbed some clean underwear. A few minutes later, Brooks knocked on my door to let me know the shower was free as he headed to the kitchen.

It was weird living with roommates since I'd been on my own for the past few years. But it wasn't completely awful. Especially when they made me food.

Once I was ready for the day, I headed into the kitchen, finding all three men sitting around the bar. It made me wonder if they ever used the actual dining room.

Grayson spotted me first, whistling as I neared. "You're going to cause a few heart attacks today, sweet stuff."

I wrinkled my nose, shaking my head at his latest nickname. I glanced down, not understanding what he meant, though. It was just a dress.

"Should I change?" I asked.

"No," all three guys said quickly in unison, then shuffled uncomfortably on their stools. Smiling to myself, I filled my plate with pancakes and bacon, taking the stool between Brooks and Grayson. They both seemed to stop what they were doing, watching me as I took a bite.

"Oh man, that's good," I said around a mouthful of pancakes.

"Thanks," Brooks said, his lips turning up at the corner.

I focused back on my plate, the others finally returning to theirs. It was quiet in the kitchen as we all ate; the only sound was the forks scraping against the plates.

"Let's go," Bubba said into the quiet, making me jump.

I quickly shoved the last of my pancake into my mouth and grabbed my bacon to go. Grayson was giving Bubba a look I couldn't decipher, but I ignored it, used to the gruffness of his words toward me.

That was alright, though. He was about to be hit with the Darcie special.

I leaned over and kissed Brooks on the cheek, taking my plate to the sink and waving over my shoulder. I could hear Grayson saying something to Brooks, whining about the kiss, making me chuckle the whole way to the garage.

Bubba was already straddling a bike, a smirk on his face. I didn't know if it was because he thought I'd be intimated or impressed. I walked around the motorcycle, taking in all the upgrades he'd done to it.

"Nice bike. Though, I probably would've gone with a V Twin engine instead. I like the sound they make."

Bubba's smile dropped, his cheeks turning red as he

shoved a helmet toward me. Taking it, I pulled my hair back first, then placed it on. I easily climbed on the back of the bike, tucking my dress in and tying it so it wouldn't fly up.

I didn't know what he expected, but I was apparently doing the opposite. I'd told him about my father being the president of the Mavericks. But I guess, like most men, he expected me to know little to nothing about bikes.

The joke was on him. I knew more about motorcycles than the truck I'd driven the day before. I wondered how confident he would've been if he'd known that. Chuckling to myself, I wrapped my arms around him, laying my head against his back.

His muscles tensed at the touch, and I felt him take a deep breath. I smiled, hoping it meant I was getting to him.

Ideas of how I could push his buttons filled my mind as he started the engine, the familiar feeling vibrating through me.

It had been so long since I'd been on a bike that I'd almost forgotten how alive it made me feel.

My legs shook as he drove, and I took a deep breath as we rode through the streets. With each turn and tilt, I got back a piece of myself I'd long forgotten—a part I hadn't realized I'd been missing until it smacked me in the face.

When we slowed, I was overwhelmed with joy from that simple ride. I could only imagine what a proper one would do to me.

Bubba parked, kicking out the kickstand. The engine shut off, allowing the world to return around us. Everything felt more. More vibrant, more intoxicating, more seductive.

He pulled off his helmet and stood from the bike, looking back at me. I didn't know what he expected to find, but it seemed it wasn't what he saw on my face.

"Are you okay? I'm sorry if I scared you. I should've taken the truck."

Holding up a hand to stop him, I pulled off the helmet, touching my cheeks in the process. I hadn't even known I'd been crying.

"I needed that more than I realized. Thank you."

Bubba swallowed, his eyes searching my face. I shook out my hair, tilting my face up toward the sun. My grin widened, and I spread my arms wide as a laugh bubbled out of me.

"God, I've missed the open road. Please tell me you have an extra bike? I need to be on two wheels. It's where I belong."

I placed my hands together in a prayer motion, hoping he'd have an answer for me.

Bubba's face changed from concern to intrigue before he blanked it, shoving all emotion away. He only grunted in response, taking both helmets and tucking them under his arm.

"Come on. Time to get to work."

Rolling my eyes, I was determined not to let his mood get to me. I would get my own bike even if it meant sacrificing the car. I'd find a way. It had felt too good to ignore how much I needed it.

Riding was part of my blood, and it was time I embraced that.

Walking in behind him, I took in the view of the shop. I hadn't been to this one, having met Lennox at the Nashville shop. Though, that store no longer existed since it had been blown up. Slade had remodeled this shop, renamed it Tattooed Hearts, and given Lennox her own suite. I was sad to be here without her, but I was happy she was living her dream.

"Wow, this place is incredible. Slade went all out," I said, taking in the chairs and lights. Bubba grunted, heading to a station in the middle. I followed, taking in the pieces of art around the place. He started to pull out some things, ignoring me, so I opened a black binder and flipped through it.

"These yours?" I asked, looking up at him.

He stopped what he was doing and looked at what I held. His jaw ticked, but he nodded, returning quickly to his setup.

"They're amazing, Bubba. You've got a lot of talent," I said honestly.

He snorted but didn't say anything else, continuing to ignore me. Rolling my eyes, I walked to the front and stopped at the front desk. The computer turned on when I moved the mouse. I glanced at the calendar, finding it similar to the program we used at the bar.

Thoughts of The Wild Horse Saloon filled me,

hating how I hadn't been able to give them any notice. By this point, I'd be a no-call no-show, and my job and reputation would be in smithereens.

I'd worked hard there to be the manager and enjoyed dancing. I hated that it was all gone now.

Part of me knew I wasn't meant to work at a bar, but it had been my home for several years, and it was hard to let it go.

Clicking on a few of the tabs, I located all the appointments for the day, who they were with, and whether they'd confirmed. I hit print so I could look at it better and make some notes since this was a new environment.

While the details printed, I found an inventory list and opened it. I hit print just as Bubba charged around the corner, a scowl on his face, his fists clenched. I'd never seen the happy-go-lucky ginger so angry before. It was such a change that it took me by surprise. Before I could think about it, my back tensed, my arms raised, and I cowered as I waited for the blow.

My body shook as I waited for the pain. When nothing happened after a few seconds, I lowered my arms. Bubba stood before me, his face stricken as he stared at me. Our eyes met, grief and anger swirling in their midst.

He turned on his heels, my arms lowering the rest of the way now that the threat of danger was gone. A door slammed in the back, causing me to jump, and I held my arms across myself as I tried to calm down.

Focusing on the things I'd printed, I looked at the first appointments and found their stations. Glancing at Bubba's, I copied the setup, pulling out the tools and utensils the artist would need. By the third station, my heart rate was back to normal, my breathing even, but there was still no sign of Bubba.

Once I had the stations completed, I took the inventory list and counted the ink bottles. It was tedious, but I found it soothing as I zoned out, singing to the song in my head as I counted. The door opened a few hours later, and I blinked, realizing how dazed I'd been.

A guy with a blue mohawk, a septum piercing, and several tattoos on display stopped in his tracks when he spotted me.

"Who are you?" he asked. He raised an eyebrow, and I realized it had a piercing in it as well.

"Darcie. Who are you?" I asked, piling on my accent.

He opened his mouth, but Bubba stepped out of the office, his eyes fixed on the man. "You're late, Dan. You'll need to set up your own station."

"No, he won't," I said, drawing the attention of both of them.

Bubba's face was hard like he was eating something difficult to chew, his jaw flexing.

"Yes, he will. I didn't show you."

"No, you didn't. But I set it up, nonetheless. Plus, the other two. I'm also done with the first page of the inventory. I'll finish the back once I call and confirm the few people who haven't yet."

Bubba blinked, his face relaxing. I smiled, twirling around and heading toward the front. I stopped, looking over my shoulder.

"I managed one of the busiest bars in Nashville, Suga. I might be blonde, but I'm a quick study." I turned to Dan, finding his eyes on me. "If you need something done differently, just let me know, and I'll make a note. I'll be here a few days a week helping out while Lennox is gone."

I smiled sweetly, then turned, walking the rest of the way to the front desk.

If anyone asked, I most definitely did not sway my hips or shake my butt. Nope. It wasn't something I'd ever do.

Lennox,

Hey girl! You've only been gone a day, and I miss you already. Have you managed to have sex in every space on the tour bus yet? If not, I expect a full report by this weekend.

So far, things have been okay. I got a phone and tablet yesterday after managing to not wreck Bubba's truck. Speaking of, did you know his name was Waylon? I think I'm going to start calling him that, just for kicks.

He's not the same guy you described or that I met that one time. I don't think he likes me very much if the grunts and scowls are any indication.

At least Grayson and Brooks have been lovely.

Speaking of... You'll never believe who Brooks turned out to be! Cowboy! The guy I fell for online is Bubba's roommate. How bizarre is that?

I don't know which I'm enjoying more... making Waylon's eye twitch each time I do something right at the shop or making his ding-dong twitch each time I bend over in my dress. Only time will tell!

Write back soon. I miss you, and I need some tips on how to piss off Waylon.

Your Bestie

CHAPTER 8

Brooks

I ROLLED the tire over to Grayson, wiping the sweat from my brow when I stopped. He lifted it up to the truck, letting out a rush of air when he secured it onto the axle. Together, we tightened the lug nuts and bolts, securing the tire to the vehicle. He nodded to the other mechanic, stepping back to wipe his face with his rag.

"It gets hotter every summer," he moaned.

Snorting, I walked over to the water cooler and filled two cups. Stepping back, I smiled before I tossed one onto his face, bringing the other to my lips.

"Hey!" he yelled but sighed as the cool water trickled down his face and soaked his shirt. "I should return the favor, but it feels too nice today."

Chuckling, I continued to drink my water, attempting to find the words I needed to say. When I wasn't on the rodeo circuit, I helped Grayson out at the shop. It was easy and gave me income when I was off.

Grayson bought this place a few years back with his earnings from modeling. He'd wanted something permanent to call his own in case the jobs quit coming or he grew tired of it.

More and more, I saw him taking fewer jobs and focusing on the shop and our brotherhood. It made me want to do the same. I just wasn't sure what outside of rodeo I was good at.

It sure as hell wasn't talking to girls. Darcie had been the first one I'd ever connected with, and that had been through a camera without ever seeing her face. I still couldn't believe she was here, in my house, just down the hall from me.

It seemed too good to be true, but I didn't think Darcie had a deceitful bone in her body, so I'd take my good fortune and thank my stars for her return to me.

"What's on your mind, Brooks? You've been quieter than usual," Grayson said, eyeing me. His hand covered the top part of his face, shielding it from the sun.

"Can we move inside?" I asked, not wanting any of the other guys to hear. They were friendly for the most part, but they weren't my brothers.

"Yeah, sure."

He called to one of the guys and led the way into the office. He sighed in relief when he stepped into the AC, an audible sound breaking free. He took his chair behind the cluttered desk, a contrast to the tidy room back at home. I'd asked him once why it was so disorganized here, and he shrugged, stating he didn't have to sleep at work.

I took the chair across from him, spreading my legs wide as I sat. Downing the last of the water, I tossed the cup into the trash before turning to look at him.

"Spit it out, Cowboy."

When Grayson really meant something, he'd call me by my road name, leaving it for only times he wanted to get his point across.

"Do you remember how you told me to try that website so I could practice talking to girls and get some," I cleared my throat, "experience?"

Grayson sat back, clearly not expecting me to say this. His brow lifted, and he nodded. "Of course. If I remember correctly, you met someone and spent a lot of money on her, then she just vanished. You were really broken up about it for months. Why?"

I fidgeted, picking at the chair arm as I rolled the words over in my head. Sometimes I had to practice saying things several times before I found the courage to utter them. A therapist had told me it was rehearsing, and while it could be helpful to decrease a lot of my anxiety, it wasn't a way to live. If I was always practicing life, I would never actually live it.

That notion had stuck with me, making me be more present with the people in my circle, knowing it was better to say something instead of only thinking it.

"Darcie," I started, instantly piquing Grayson's interest. I'd seen how he watched her this morning, jealous of the kiss she'd given me. It was why I wanted to talk with him, so he'd know.

"Yeah, she's a sweet thing," he said, a smile crossing his face. "You have a thing for her?"

I nodded, licking my lips. "I do. She's the girl."

His brow furrowed as he focused on me. "I think she's pretty great, but you just met her, Brooks. I wouldn't go and make any proclamations to her. You'll scare her away."

I smiled, able to appreciate his concern for me. There had been a time in my life when I hadn't had anyone care about me. Finding Bubba and Pretty Boy had been the thing that saved me.

"No, I mean, she's the girl from the website. She's my Rose."

He stopped, staring at me for a few seconds. I was worried he wasn't breathing until he finally blinked. His face was blank, making me wonder if I had misread his interest.

"Wow, okay. That's big. Um, yeah. That's great."

Grayson fiddled with something on his desk, putting the documents and order slips into piles. It was his nervous tick coming out, his need to clean and organize.

"Grayson, you might want to hear what I have to say before you jump to conclusions."

He stopped, his eyes lifting to mine. "What do you mean? I remember how you felt about her. I'm guessing you'll be riding off into the sunset now?"

I shook my head, a small smile lifting at the corner of

my mouth. It warmed my heart that he would let her go for me. He truly was my brother.

"No. I think she's the one we've all been waiting for."

Grayson's eyes searched mine, his jaw flexing as he processed what I said. "I don't understand. If she's the girl you've been hung up on, why would you..." He stopped, waving his arms in front of him. "You know. I don't get it. Besides, we talked about that late one night when we were all drunk. I didn't think any of us meant it for real."

"So if the perfect girl walked into the shop and we all liked her, you wouldn't want to try to keep us together? You'd brush it off as drunken conversation?"

Grayson's mouth opened and closed, at a loss for words. Finally, he opened his mouth, an argument on his tongue. "This isn't that. You had a relationship with her. You have a right to claim her."

"And if I believed she was the perfect woman to fit all three of our needs, to have that balance of light and dark, and the capacity to love us all, you'd still tell me no?" I challenged.

He was quiet for a while, the gears rolling in his head.

"You really think Darcie is that?" he asked quietly.

"I do. I think I always did. Every time I talked to her, I wished you and Waylon could as well. She made everything better, and I knew we needed someone like her. And this morning, I saw the way you both looked at her. Though Waylon is fighting his attraction."

Grayson snorted, nodding. "Yeah. He thinks he's too

old for her. But I caught the fire in his eyes. I hadn't seen it there in a while, either."

I nodded, feeling more hopeful now that Grayson seemed on board. "And you were jealous she gave me attention. I saw you watching her every move. She intrigues you."

"There's something about her. I won't deny that." He chuckled, rubbing his brow. "I'm pretty sure she went into my room yesterday and switched around my things. I opened my drawer to put on socks and found shirts. I about had a conniption until I smelled her fragrance lingering in the air. Then all I could do was smile and laugh at her playful behavior."

"That sounds like Darcie," I sighed, my smile growing bigger.

"Do you really think it could work? The three of us and her? Will she go for it?"

I shrugged. "She's best friends with Lennox, so we have that on our side. She's aware of this type of relationship, so it won't be a completely new thing for her. And I think she will. I could tell she liked the attention from all of us."

"Liking attention and wanting to be sexual with three men are two different things, Brooks."

"Yeah, yeah. I just have a hunch."

"How are we going to get Bubba on board?" he asked, narrowing his eyes.

"I'm not sure we'll have to do much. I think we need to talk to Darcie first, and she'll do the rest. Besides,

Bubba's already halfway there. Listen to this text he sent me."

I pulled out my phone and read it off.

Waylon: This girl is driving me nuts.

Me: How so?

Waylon: She wants a motorcycle.

Me: Why is that bad?

Waylon: She'll get herself killed.

Me: Then teach her how not to. But I think she might surprise you.

Waylon: The less time I have to spend with her, the better. You guys are taking her tomorrow.

Me: Is the big bad biker scared of a little girl?

Waylon: She's definitely not a little girl.

I looked up, catching Grayson's eyes. He had a knowing look, his smile wide as he peered back at me.

"You're right. Okay, maybe you're not so crazy after all."

"Shy, yes. Crazy, never."

We both laughed, and that feeling of excitement I got before the gate was lifted at the rodeo spread through me. My phone buzzed, and I glanced down to see Waylon had sent another text.

> Waylon: Shit, I think I messed up.

> Me: Why? What happened?

I instantly went on high alert, both for my brother and the girl I had feelings for.

> Waylon: I was angry and came around the corner, not thinking. She flinched, cowering in front of me like she expected me to hit her. I fucked up, man.

Sweat dripped down my back as I tried to imagine what Darcie was feeling. From everything she'd told me last night, I was worried this would push her away.

> Me: You gotta apologize.

> Waylon: How?

> Me: Looks like you're teaching her how to drive your bike on the way home tonight.

> Waylon: Fuck.

I laughed, catching Grayson's attention.

"What now?" he asked, finishing straightening the last pile. His desk did look better. I wondered if the threat of sending her here tomorrow had motivated him to make it more organized.

"Waylon scared her, so I told him to apologize by teaching her how to ride." My eyes sparkled as I chuckled to myself. I knew Darcie could ride; she told me how she'd basically been raised on them. I wished I could be there to see Bubba's face. "She grew up in an MC. She's no stranger to bikes."

"Oh man, that's going to be a riot. I wish we had a camera," Grayson said, mirroring my thoughts.

"Maybe if we hurry, we can get there before they leave," I suggested.

Grayson looked at the clock, then the schedule, jumping up from the desk. "Chop, chop, Cowboy. We have a girl to woo."

Grinning, I hopped up, a new skip in my step. I knew I could've been selfish and kept Darcie to myself. But the dream we'd conjured up one drunken night had stayed with me; the hope we could always be a brotherhood with one woman to devote ourselves to felt right.

There hadn't been any women before that had fit the bill. Mostly because I'd always been too shy to step outside my comfort zone and try. With Darcie, it wasn't as scary; her body was already a permanent image in my mind.

As we finished the day, I couldn't help but notice how much happier Grayson seemed too. Darcie would be good for us, and we'd keep her safe.

In the back of my mind, I knew I'd have to face the ghost of Maddox with her one day, but for now, I'd relish in the fact that the girl of my dreams was no longer just a voice over a screen.

Diary #8

Dear Mom,

I had an incident today where I was taken back to that moment in my life when I felt my weakest. It lasted only a few seconds, but it was enough to make me stop and question myself.

Am I not as strong as I thought?

Why was this still affecting me?

I hate that Agonizer has scarred my life and left his imprint on my soul. I want nothing to do with the man, but it's there, a lasting bruise that will never heal.

I need to do something that makes me feel strong. I need to keep fighting, so I don't revert back to that version of me.

I said I would learn to protect myself, so it's time I put my money where my mouth is and remember all my training.

I'll be okay. I know that. I just needed to remind myself for a moment.

Love,

Me

CHAPTER 9

Darcie

BY THE END of the day, I felt accomplished and proud of my work. I'd made friends with a few of the artists, learning how they wanted their trays set up. Bubba had avoided me, only giving me grunts when I asked for his opinion.

I could feel his eyes on me, though, causing me to purposely bend over and flirt with the others when he was watching. The number of items he dropped made me question his ability to tattoo. I'd worry about his skill if I hadn't seen his work.

"See you guys later," I hollered as I stepped outside after Bubba's shift was over. His face was blank, but I caught him fidgeting with the keys. "Everything okay?" I asked, curious about his sudden nervousness.

He kept walking, a grunt leaving him before he cleared his throat. "I um," he started, rubbing the back of his neck. Bubba turned, his eyes meeting mine for the first time in hours. I crossed my arms over my chest, feeling like I needed some protection.

"I wanted to apologize for earlier. I didn't mean to frighten you. I'd never hurt you, Darcie."

I took a deep breath, nodding as I let it out. "I know. It wasn't you. It's just..." I waved my hands around in front of me. "Men haven't always been the nicest to me." I left it at that, not wanting to get into my trauma in the parking lot.

Bubba's face changed from contrite to rage. "Who?" he growled.

"It's in the past. It doesn't matter." I dropped my arms, fiddling with my hem.

His nostrils flared, his jaw tightening. I couldn't understand why he reacted the way he did. He hadn't even known me back then.

"I'm sorry I made you remember, then. I'd like to make it up to you." He let out a pained breath. It instantly made me focus on him, not on my feelings.

"Oh?"

"Yes. I'm not going to buy you a bike, but I'll teach you."

"Teach... me?" I asked, a smile spreading across my face.

"Yeah. You have to learn the right way. How to be safe. A bike isn't something to get on a whim. After I'm satisfied you know how to handle yourself, then and only then will I think about taking you to look at one. Understand?"

Bubba looked so serious it was hard not to smile. Oh, this was going to be fun.

"But what if it's hard?" I asked coyly, twirling the hair around my finger. My smile wanted to break free, so I bit my lip to contain it.

"That's why I'm teaching you," he said, his voice deeper.

He went through the basic steps on which handle was the accelerator and which was the brake. I climbed on and put the helmet on, going through the same routine with my dress. I heard him cuss as it hiked up my legs, but it was better than it flying everywhere.

"On second thought, I changed my mind. This is a horrible idea," he started. I ignored him, kicking the kickstand and turning the keys. He went to reach for me, but I just smiled, waved, and took off.

I heard him shouting about two hands, but I sped up, the feel of the bike already making me feel whole again. The smooth leather against my legs, the heat of the exhaust, and the vibration were nearly enough to make me orgasm on the spot.

I did a few laps around the parking lot, watching Waylon as he shook his head, a smile growing with each pass. When I had enough of punishing him, I pulled up and stopped, pulling the helmet off and shaking out my hair.

"Motorcycle princess, remember?" I teased.

Something akin to heat flashed in his eyes before it

vanished. One corner of his mouth tilted up as he looked at me. He shook his head, sighing.

"Did I pass, Waylon?" I taunted. He chuckled, his whole chest moving with the action.

"I guess I deserved that. Am I forgiven?"

"Yep. Though, I'm holding you to take me to get one. Slade said he'd sell my car and I want to use that for a bike. It's been too long since I've had a real piece of machinery between my legs." I winked, and I would've sworn I saw his cheeks heat. I stared, waiting for him to say something.

"Can I have my bike back now?" he asked, ignoring my comment.

"I dunno. She rides pretty smoothly. I might need another lap."

"Fine, I promise to take you on the weekend. We can get something cheap, and the guys can help fix it up if you want."

"Yes!" I cheered, fist-pumping the air. I tossed the key back, sliding to the back. "Let's go, Big Guy."

He rolled his eyes but hiked his leg over the seat, situating himself. Putting on my helmet, I wrapped my arms around him, feeling him suck in a breath again.

I smiled to myself, knowing I was getting to him. I conveniently ignored the part of me that enjoyed it for more than entertainment.

He took off, taking the curves a little more danger-ously this time, leaning into them more than he had on the way here. I cheered and hollered after each one, feeling him chuckle at my enthusiasm.

When we returned, the other two bikes and trucks were parked at the house. As odd as it was to miss the other guys, I had. I jumped off the bike, tossing the helmet to Bubba as I undid my dress and ran inside.

Brooks and Grayson were in the kitchen, gathered around the stove. At my entrance, they looked up, and I grinned wide, doing a little jig as I neared.

"I took Bubba's bike out, and now we're going to look at some this weekend. You guys get to help!" I shouted, spinning and twirling. I was so hyped up from my ride, I probably wasn't making sense.

"What now?" Brooks asked, returning my smile.

Grayson took my hands and spun me into a twirl before bringing me back to dip. I laughed, the sound flowing freely as we continued to dance around the kitchen.

"You're good at that," I said once he stopped. My chest rose with each breath I took, my face hurting from all the smiling.

"So are you." His eyes roamed over my face, his lips curving up as he looked at me. It felt like he was seeing me for something more this time. He winked, letting me go as Bubba stomped into the kitchen.

He narrowed his eyes at Brooks, pointing a finger.

"I'm this tempted to put you on trash duty for an extra week," he barked.

Grayson and Brooks doubled over laughing, tears

falling down their cheeks. Brooks finally calmed himself, wiping his face.

"It worked, though, didn't it?" he asked, lifting his brow at Bubba.

I watched the exchange between them, wondering what it was about. Bubba looked at me, his eyes softening a little before he walked over and punched Brooks in the arm.

Grayson just laughed harder until Bubba glared, and he straightened up, stepping back and pulling me in front of him.

"You think she'll stop me?" he asked, dropping his eyes to me.

I smiled sweetly, batting my eyelashes. I wasn't sure exactly what was going on, but since my mission was to give Bubba shit, it aligned for the moment.

He stopped, cursed, and spun on his heels as he stomped out of the kitchen. The other two broke out in more laughter, apparently finding it just as hilarious to mess with Bubba as I did.

"So, what's for dinner?" I asked, hopping onto the counter. "Do you need any help?"

"From a pretty girl, always!" Grayson sang, sashaying his hips over to me. "How was your day, sunflower?"

"It was a lot better than I expected. I liked meeting all the artists, and I felt like I helped. Their system was easy to understand."

"How about you help me out at the garage tomorrow?" he asked, wiggling his eyebrows.

"Hmm, does helping out involve sexual favors?" I teased.

He stopped, his mouth opening and closing before he cleared it, leaning against the counter near me.

"It can," he purred, sending shivers down my spine.

I slapped him. "If you need actual help, then I'm game. I just don't fancy being part of a cheesy porno, where you ask me if there's anything your big wrench can fix."

Brooks sputtered, a laugh bellowing out of him. Grayson froze, his face turning a little red as he blinked at me.

"Where have you been all my life, Darcie?" he asked. I laughed, smacking his arm. Though I played it off as a joke, the look on his face and the softness of his voice made me reconsider.

"Oh, here, there, everywhere," I replied. "But I'm here now." I dropped my voice, almost whispering the last part. His smile softened as he watched me. Bending down, I dropped a kiss on his forehead before jumping off the counter and moving toward Brooks.

I wrapped my arms around his waist without thinking. It felt too nice to hug him now that I could.

He stopped what he was doing, turning so he could look at me. His fingers brushed my hair back, his eyes roaming my face for something.

"I'm glad you had a good day, sweetheart," he whispered. I noticed how his ears turned a little pink. It was cute how nervous he still was at times. I liked it about him, though.

"Sorry if you're not a hugger. I just really wanted one."

"I'll always take one from you."

We stared at one another, lost in the moment, until a throat cleared, bringing us back to Earth.

"Don't burn dinner," Grayson said, pulling some plates out of the cabinet.

Brooks squeezed me before letting me go, focusing back on the food he was preparing.

"What are you making?" I asked, pulling open a few drawers until I found the silverware. I could never remember where they were.

"Cowboy sloppy joes."

"Never had them. Sounds good."

"I'm not as good of a cook as Grayson. It's edible, though," he replied, turning off the burner and opening a drawer.

"I'm sure you're underselling yourself," I said. "Breakfast was great."

"Yeah, well, that's a bit easier."

"What else do we need?" I asked, looking around the kitchen. Grayson had set the table in the dining room. He shouted for Bubba, who walked in, stopping when he noticed it.

"What are you doing?" he asked.

"Eating dinner," he said, widening his eyes. "Like grownups."

I moved over to the glasses, smiling as I filled them with the tea sitting out. It was obvious they were doing this for me. It was too sweet to tell them they didn't have to.

Carrying two glasses over, I sat them down before returning for the other two. When I returned, I noticed how they were all standing, looking at one another.

"Are we going to sit?" I asked, not understanding.

"You first," Brooks said, eyeing the others.

Narrowing my eyes, I took a seat, the others following immediately. There was a little shoving as they claimed the chairs, and I smiled bigger. Having a few guys fight over who sat next to you never hurt a girl's ego.

Bubba ignored Brooks and Grayson, taking a seat at the head of the table. Eventually, Brooks landed next to me, making Grayson sit across.

"This is better anyway," he said, picking up his fork. "I can stare at Darcie's beautiful face all night."

Grinning, I winked, thanking him for the compliment. Brooks grumbled something but picked up the food and served us. It was such an odd experience; I didn't know how to feel.

It had been so long since I'd had a family dinner. The last one hadn't gone as planned. Since then, it mainly had been me on my own, so I ate wherever I wanted.

"Thank you," I said, scooping some food onto my fork.

Dinner was quiet; the guys were clearly not used to sitting altogether. I asked them questions about their day, joining in when I had a funny moment to share about Bubba. By the end, even Bubba was smiling and relaxed as they shared. It felt nice and something I'd miss.

"Thank you for dinner. I'm going to do some research for a bit. I'll do the dishes or whatever my chore is after, if that's okay."

Bubba watched me, an emotion I didn't know crossing his face. "Of course. Dishes would be helpful. Thank you, Darcie."

Nodding, I left the table, placing my dish in the sink. As I walked by, I found them huddled together, gossiping like school girls. They stopped when I neared, so I waved, continuing down the hallway.

Part of me wanted to stop and eavesdrop, but the more pressing matter of finding Maddox weighed on me, pushing me down the hall.

Diary #9

Dear Maddox,

I had a moment today where I wasn't thinking about you, and it scared me. I didn't expect to like where I am so much. These guys are showing me things I didn't think I could feel anymore.

If you were here, it might just be perfect.

That might sound weird, but it would. I know things with us have been broken for a while, but I never stopped loving you. I don't think I know how.

I didn't expect to ever like anyone else the way I did you, but I'm starting to.

These guys are different. They're good people. I think you'd get along great with them, honestly.

I might be wishing for too much, but since this is my diary and you'll never read it, I can.

I rode again today, and it was marvelous. I'm going to do it again. I need to. I think stopping was a mistake.

Even though I know why I did, now I wonder if I hadn't, if I would've stayed away so long. Maybe that was the point.

Things are changing, though. I feel different. I feel stronger.

I'm getting to be the Darcie I always believed I was.

I hope you get to meet her. I think you'd love her even more.

Love,

Darcie

CHAPTER 10

Darcie

I SPENT an hour searching the MCD database before giving up. Maddox hadn't logged into the server for a while. I spotted a few entries from my father, but as usual, none were for me. I didn't know if it was frustrating or comforting knowing he was checking in on me. I wished he'd reach out and speak with me. Maybe then I could process some of the anger I had toward him.

Tossing my tablet onto the bed, I lay back with a groan.

"Everything okay?" Brooks asked from the doorway.

I turned my head, taking him in. I smiled at him, beckoning him in.

"I'm trying to find Maddox. I looked through our database, but he hasn't been on in years. I don't know what to try next."

Brooks smirked, walked closer to me, and sat on the bed. "May I?" he asked.

Nodding, I leaned up on my elbows as he picked up my tablet. He typed in a few things before stopping to look at me.

"Last name?" he asked.

"King."

"Do you know what state he was in last?"

"Georgia, I believe."

He hit a few more keys on the tablet and then turned it toward me. "That him?"

I sat up, grabbed the tablet, and stared at the mugshot. I swallowed, nodding. "How? Where?" I asked, glancing up with tears in my eyes. It was overwhelming having found him.

"There's actually a prison database. You just need their name and state, and you can find anyone."

"Oh." My cheeks heated, the obvious solution staring me in the face.

"Don't be embarrassed. It's cute you didn't know. Means you've never had to use it before."

I wiped my eyes, nodding. "Thanks, Brooks."

"Of course."

I glanced back down, reading the information. "Wait, does this mean he's out?" I asked. Turning the tablet around, I pointed to a line. Brooks peered closer, his brows furrowing as he concentrated.

"Hmm, it could be a couple of things. He might have just been transferred. But it doesn't look like he's in that prison anymore."

The hope I had sank as I faced another dead end. If

he was out, why hadn't he come to me? Despite knowing he had no idea where I was, our love felt like something you could feel at times, manifesting a path from me to him.

"At least I know."

Brooks watched me, concern washing over his features. "Hey, I'm sure if he could, he'd get in touch. He doesn't know your number or address, right?"

I nodded, realizing how dumb I was being. I couldn't tell Brooks how I felt; it always felt like Maddox intrinsically knew where I was. We'd never needed addresses or phones before. We just found our way to one another.

"Yeah, you're right. I'm being silly."

"No, you're not. Could you leave a message on that database you mentioned?"

My eyes shot up to his, a smile growing. Excitedly, I hugged him, almost falling into his lap in my exuberance.

"Oof," he said, chuckling.

"You're a genius, Brooks. Thanks. Seriously. Most men wouldn't be so kind to help me find an old boyfriend."

"He wasn't just a boyfriend, though, was he?"

I shook my head, dropping my eyes. "No. He wasn't. How are you okay with this?"

He sighed, his thumb coming up to cup my cheek. "That's one of the things I wanted to talk to you about. Is now a good time?"

"Absolutely. Let me just leave this first before I forget."

His ears were a little red, but he nodded, letting me sit back on the bed. I signed back into the site, leaving a message on our old message board.

> Rosebud: I took a trip to visit a friend. The air tastes too of envy, Darling. How everyone always responds to summer is killing me.

I chuckled at my nonsense message but knew he'd get it. It was the MCD code, after all, to use the first letter of each word. Hopefully he would understand it from there. I sat the tablet down and scooted closer to Brooks.

"Did you want to talk here?" I asked, grabbing his hand.

"Yeah. It works." He swallowed, his eyes roaming my face. I smiled, hoping to encourage him.

"What I'm going to say might sound crazy, but I hope you'll hear me out." I nodded, rubbing my thumb across his palm. "Before I met Grayson and Waylon, I never fit in. I was always on the outside, never belonging. I grew up in foster care and was shuffled from home to home. When I turned eighteen, I was given a bus ticket and two hundred dollars. I had no idea what I was going to do. I found an ad in a paper for a rodeo school. I'd always loved horses, so I thought I'd give it a shot. I met Grayson after one show. He had been there to promote one of the brands. I was sitting alone at the bar, trying to get up the nerve to talk to a girl."

He chuckled, shaking his head at the memory.

"We got to talking, and I realized he was one of the first people I didn't feel awkward around. Grayson just has that way about him. He makes everyone feel comfortable. We exchanged numbers, and I promised to reach out if I was ever in the area. When I graduated from rodeo school, I felt more lost than before I'd started. I was on the road, constantly traveling from rodeo to rodeo, and I felt so alone. One night, when I was feeling really low, I messaged Grayson. From there, our friendship grew. He doesn't know this, but he saved me. He helped me feel like I belonged. I eventually came through town and met Waylon. He became like a big brother to me instantly. He taught me how to drive a motorcycle and everything about them."

He smiled down at me, pure happiness radiating through his eyes.

"When they asked me if I wanted to be part of the Brotherhood, I didn't hesitate. I felt like I belonged here. Something I'd been searching for my whole life. Rodeo is a job for now, but these guys are my brothers for life."

"I know what you mean. It's what I love about the MC life. People outside of it don't get it. But I do. There's nothing more powerful than that feeling of family and belonging. It was one of the hardest parts of having to leave it. I didn't just lose my dad, but my road family too."

"So this might not sound so crazy to you then," he started, clearing his throat. "There used to be a fourth member of our Brotherhood. Jackson. He was closer to

Waylon's age. They'd grown up together and were close. When he left, it created this void in us, Waylon the most."

"Why did he leave?" I asked, curious.

"I'm getting there, sweetheart." He smiled at me, making my insides warm. I mimed zipping my lips, making him chuckle.

"Jackson met a woman he wanted to make his old lady. He didn't know how to do that and be in the club. Ours is a bit different in that we only have a few of us who are actual members. Some guys in town and the next hang out at the local bar and will ride with us on occasion. The four of us shared everything like you've probably seen. We shared the bills, meals, and chores. We shared our problems and dreams. Jackson didn't know how to fit his new dream into that model. So, he eventually left. You're in his room, actually."

I looked around but couldn't find any traces of the man who'd been there.

"While we understood why he left, it was a hard blow. One night, the three of us were drinking and talking. We were trying to find a solution, one where we didn't end up in the same situation. None of us wanted to leave the others. I joked that, as a group, we'd be the perfect man for one woman. I had the sweet side, Grayson the smooth side, and Waylon the protector side. I'd thrown it out there as a joke, but then we all started thinking about it and realized it was the perfect solution. If we could all fall in love with the same woman, we wouldn't have to break up our Brotherhood."

I blinked, not having expected that explanation.

"So, you're saying that if I date you, then I can only be long-term if I'm willing to date the others?"

Brooks paled, his eyes going wide. "No, I mean. I don't think I'm explaining this correctly." He took a breath, squeezing my hand. "I like you a lot, Darcie. You're my dream girl. In fact, I never thought I'd ever be able to meet someone as amazing as you, much less talk to them. The fact you like me as well blows my mind. And if I'm honest, if there was ever someone to make me willing to leave the guys for, it would be you. But I can't deny the chemistry I see between you and each of them. I'm not saying you have to date them, too, just that I think you'd be the perfect woman for us. I could never deny my brothers the happiness I think you could give them."

I stared at him, a bit stunned. I'd joked with Lennox about getting my own harem, but I never expected it despite my feelings for multiple men. I didn't know why. Probably my belief no one ever stayed. What was the point in worrying about complicated feelings if they were never around long? It was a ridiculous way to live, but I hadn't really been doing much of that either.

Brooks was showing me how I could change that. How I could live in the moment and the future. It sounded scary, but I couldn't deny I was interested.

"Have you talked to the other two? Are they on

board with this? Because I don't think Waylon likes me like that. I'm more of an annoying kid sister to him."

I said the words, despite knowing they weren't true. It felt too real to admit the attraction between us just yet.

Brooks's lips tilted up to the side, his brows lifting. He didn't say anything, just gave me that look. I squirmed under his gaze, too stubborn to back down.

"We both know that isn't true, sweetheart. He wouldn't have let you ride his bike if he didn't care about you. He's only let one other person on it since he got it, and that was only because Grayson was working on it."

My mouth dropped open, shocked at what he said. Deep down, I knew what he said was true. A man and their motorcycle were a sacred thing. I hadn't even blinked when he gave me the keys. I'd been away from the club too long.

At least that was my excuse and not the growing feelings in my belly for the brute.

"I'm not saying I'm on board, but where would Maddox fit? I don't know where things are with us, but I'm not sure I could close the door."

He sighed, nodding. "I know. And that's something we'll discuss when he returns. For now, I just need to know if you're interested in this."

I thought over everything he said. It didn't make me feel like I would be used like a sweet butt, passed around from one member to the next. Instead, they wanted to avoid all that and share a woman. I did find Waylon and Grayson attractive; the chemistry between us was electric.

I didn't know if it would turn into anything more, but that wasn't what he was asking me.

"Just to be clear, you're asking if I'd be interested in dating all three of you and seeing where it goes? I'm not making a commitment or anything to be your club whore?"

Brooks reared back, shaking his head. "Never. You'd be our queen."

His voice held so much reverence that I believed him. It sent tingles over my body at the promise in his words.

"Are the others on board with this?"

He cringed, his eyes moving toward the door. Grayson appeared, a smile on his face.

"I am," he said as he walked over, plopping down next to me. His whole body touched mine, and I bit the inside of my cheek to stop it from showing just how much I liked it.

Okay, so maybe there was no denying I found him attractive. Our touch alone was igniting things in me.

"As for Bubba," Grayson started, "he's going to deny himself and push you away. You're already under his skin, so it won't take long if you keep trying. Plus, I think it will be fun to push his buttons, don't you?"

I chuckled, nodding. "Yeah. I do have a passion for making the Viking ginger tick."

The guys laughed, something passing between them. Grayson picked up my other hand, his eyes caressing my face as he looked at me.

"I know this isn't conventional, Darcie. But if you

gave it a try, I think it could be amazing. I think you're gorgeous, hilarious, and sweet. You fit in with us so well. I doubt you even realize it. So give us a chance to show you."

I licked my lips, his words bringing goosebumps to my skin. "Okay. I'm willing to be open and try."

Grayson leveled me with a megawatt smile, almost knocking me over with its magnitude. I fully understood how he got modeling gigs. The boy was too pretty for his own good.

"I shall leave you then. I look forward to tomorrow, and perhaps after work, you'll let me take you dancing?"

"Dancing, huh? I'd like that." My face naturally lit up, the fun and joy he brought to the room bleeding over onto me. I couldn't help but smile in his presence.

He leaned over and kissed my cheek before hopping off the bed and sauntering out of the room. I watched him, unable to take my eyes off his ass.

Brooks chuckled, pulling me back to the moment.

My cheeks heated at being caught. "That doesn't make you jealous?" I asked, curious how it worked.

"No. It really doesn't, at least with my brothers."

I nodded, understanding in a way. Brooks leaned forward, his lips nearing mine.

"Can I kiss you now, Darcie?"

I nodded, my eyes fluttering closed as he bridged the distance. Brooks's lips were soft as they touched mine. He pressed into me but didn't do anything else. I knew he'd been shy with girls, but I didn't know what that translated to. Had he kissed anyone before? Had he done more?

It was something I'd want to know later, but for now, I enjoyed the sweet kiss, storing it away as a perfect first kiss.

"Night, Darcie."

"Night, Cowboy," I whispered, not wanting to break the magic of the moment.

He walked out, stopping at the door to look back. I smiled, the feeling more natural the longer I was around them.

Laying back on the bed, I giggled to myself as happiness filled me.

Diary #10

Lennox,

Oh my god! You won't believe what's happened. I'm still not believing it, and it happened to me!

Apparently, you started a trend.

The guys... they want to share me.

I'm still unsure how it will work, but I'm down for the ride.

Bubba's in the dark, so I'll have fun teasing him until he breaks. Any tips?

Brooks kissed me, and it was the sweetest thing ever. Grayson wants to take me dancing tomorrow. Would it be wrong of me to go further with him than I have with Brooks if the opportunity presented itself?

Do I need to keep them on the same level? Go in order? Just how does that work? Is it more of a sex roulette? Whoever it lands on gets the position?

Speaking of positions... you need to spill. I'm suddenly very curious about multiple partner experiences.

In other news, nothing from Maddox. I'm hopeful, though. It might be dumb of me to be so, but I am.

I also haven't heard anything about Chase. I think I'm scared to look. But there haven't been any news bulletins calling for my arrest, either. I don't know if that's good or bad. Preparing for trouble is hard if you don't know what's coming.

Speaking of coming... How many orgasms have you had at one time? Ballpark figure?

Call me, text me, or write back soon. Your girl needs all the deets.

Love,

Your soon-to-be harem sister (but not like in a weird way).

CHAPTER 11

Grayson

DARCIE HUMMED along as she restocked filters in the supply room, shaking her butt as she rocked to the tune. The short shorts she wore made my dick hard every time I looked at her, imagining my hands on her. I fully understood why Bubba had struggled to have her around him all day. She was an unintentional dick tease.

Or maybe it was intentional. With Darcie, it was hard to say.

She was a whirlwind of energy, floating around in a cloud of sunshine. I hadn't wanted to admit how right Cowboy had been. She was perfect for us.

She didn't let me get away with my shit and liked to play just as much. She was sweet and soft with Cowboy and pushed Bubba to get out of his head. She was dynamite wrapped in a blonde package that I, for one, couldn't wait to unwrap.

Any potential burns would be worth it.

"You like to sing?" I asked, realizing I wanted to get to know her. Not just her body but her soul.

Okay, that was deep, and I was starting to weird myself out.

Thankfully, Darcie didn't seem to notice as she spun, a grin on her face.

"Not really. Just for fun. I'm more into the dance side of things."

Eyebrows lifting, I leaned forward, intrigued. Dancing was a passion of mine. It was why I was taking her tonight. It showed a side of me I liked the most.

"What kind of dancing?" I asked.

"All kinds. I worked at the Wild Horse Saloon, so for the past few years, it's mostly been line dancing, but I can do a range of things. Just not ballet or tap, and hip hop isn't my strongest."

I laughed, shaking my head. "And here I thought I was smooth asking you to go dancing, prepared to show you all my best moves."

"Who says you still can't? I'm interested in what you consider your best, Pretty Boy."

Heat rose in me, the desire to show her right now strong.

"Speaking of tonight," she hedged, giving me a wink. "Would it be possible to stop and get some different clothes? I only have about three outfits, and you've seen them already."

"If I'm doing things right, there won't be much need for clothes," I teased.

Her ears turned red, and I liked that I could affect her as much as she did me.

"Hm, that sounds tempting, but I'm trying not to get arrested for the time being, so perhaps some clothes to start would be wise."

"Fine. You win," I said, chuckling. "There are a few places we could go on lunch if you wanted?"

"Yes, that would be perfect. Thank you, Grayson."

She smiled in a way that made it feel like it was only for me. I knew I was in trouble if I was already feeling this way after only a few days—like she could be the one.

"I'm done with the restocking. Want me to take a look at the online system?" she asked.

I cringed, worried she'd think differently of me if she saw the office. "Um, sure. Just know it's a work in progress."

I stood up and walked her through the shop, the guys stopping to watch her walk by. I narrowed my eyes at them, warning them all to knock it off. Brooks stood and blocked their view as well, his usual calm demeanor over-ridden by his need to shield her.

"Whoa, okay, I see what you mean. You sure this is your office?" she teased, turning her head back toward me.

I cringed, rubbing the back of my neck. My face felt warm, so I tried to play it off.

"Yeah, well, contrary to popular belief, I don't bring girls here."

Her face fell, and I realized my mistake. "Shit, I don't

mean I bring girls back to the house. That's a rule, actually. I was just trying to play off my messiness when it's not my stuff. Bills and order forms aren't my forte, so they kind of pile up until I'm forced to deal with them. Brooks put in a fancy system, but I'm not great at using it."

"Ooo, a project!" She smiled, clapping her hands, the earlier sadness dissipating.

I sighed in relief. I needed to remember that my games didn't work with Darcie. She wanted my truth. It wasn't something I'd ever given a person outside of the Brotherhood. While that was scary within itself, it also felt worthwhile.

In the few days I'd known her, she'd shown me I was more than just a "pretty boy" to her.

"Have at it. If you can make sense of this mess, I'll buy you all the clothes you could want."

She raised her eyebrows, a smirk playing on her lips. "That's a challenge I can get behind. You might regret that; I love a good organizational project."

I showed Darcie the system and what the logins were, then shut the door behind me, walking back out into the garage. The men stopped talking as they watched me. I took a bet in my head who'd be the first to say something. Ten seconds later, I wasn't wrong.

"So, what's the deal with the blonde?" Rodger asked.

I debated what to say. I knew it might be presumptuous to call her mine, but I didn't want any of these fools thinking they had a chance, either.

"She's off limits. Let's leave it at that," I said, glaring at all the guys.

Rodger tossed his hands, smirking as he returned to the engine he was working on. The other guys followed suit, and I let out a breath I hadn't realized I'd been holding. Brooks sauntered over, chuckling as he neared.

"You think that's going to work?" he asked.

"If it doesn't, they'll regret it," I growled. The thought of one of them being with Darcie made my anger boil. I'd only kissed the girl, and I was already possessive as fuck.

"How's it going, otherwise?" he asked.

"Good, I think. She seems to believe she'll be able to make heads and tails of my system. I promised to buy her clothes in return. She wants to go shopping at lunch. I might need you to take her so I can get caught up here. You okay with that?"

"Get an hour to spend with Darcie alone? Hell, yes." Cowboy smiled, and I noticed he'd been doing that more than ever since she'd appeared.

I didn't need any more confirmation she was the one for us. The three of us were already changing, molding ourselves to surround her.

Brooks slapped my back, leaving me to the car I was working on as he returned to his. I turned up the music, needing something to keep my mind off the beautiful bombshell behind my desk.

I was finally closing time, and I couldn't wait to get out of here. The garage was typically my place of solace. Where I could let go of the perfect control I had over every other aspect of my life. I could get my hands dirty here without it being the end of the world. This place had saved me in a lot of ways.

But today, the only thing I could think about was my date with Darcie.

Gearing up enough courage, I stepped into my office and stopped, amazed at what I saw.

"What? How?" I asked. My eyes grew large as I turned, taking in the room. Every ounce of paper was gone, the desk clear. It made the office feel bigger, and I recognized a picture of the three of us.

"It wasn't as bad as it looked. You had things in piles. Once I figured out your system, I could manipulate that for you in the program. Would you like to see it?"

I stared at her, gobsmacked by what she was telling me. I didn't believe her for one second that it had been easy. My office had become the place I refused to let any of my mother's tendencies touch, justifying that it was a garage and therefore meant to be messy.

Walking over to the desk, I realized how limiting that had been. Maybe I didn't need to be as controlled and clean here, but going completely without only invited chaos.

"I know you got a few things earlier, but now I'm buying you a whole store," I said once she'd shown me how she'd set up the folders. It made sense when she explained it.

"I don't think I need a whole store, but I'll definitely take you up on a few new things. I'm using my money for my bike. Bubba said you'd help fix it up if it needed."

"Damn straight. Besides, I wouldn't let you ride anything until I'd looked it over, Sunflower." My voice dropped, the sound deep as I stared into her eyes. Something I hadn't noticed before swirled in them, and I leaned forward, the magnetic pull between us too great.

"Ready to go?" Cowboy asked, slapping the door. I jumped back, sending him a glare. I knew he saw what I was about to do and purposefully interrupted.

"Yep. I can't wait to wear my new dress and dance with you, Laws."

"Laws?" I asked, my eyes returning to hers.

"It's my name for you. It suits you better. You're my Laws."

I didn't know what she meant by that, but I'd be her anything if she asked.

The ride home was quiet as I shifted in the truck. The anticipation of the night was bearing down on me, and I was worried I'd crumble under it.

Darcie ran to her room when we returned to the

house with a bag. Bubba wasn't there yet, so I told Brooks I'd see him later.

Taking a shower, I took my time to shave and use all my best products. I wanted to smell and look good for Darcie tonight. Putting on a button-down shirt, I left the top buttons open as I slid on a pair of worn-in jeans that cupped my butt. Tossing on an old cowboy hat and boots, I sprayed myself with my cologne before heading out the door.

Girls tended to think guys didn't care about their appearance or put as much effort into it as women did. I was here to tell you that some guys did. Perhaps my upbringing and background in the modeling industry played a part, but I'd be the first to admit that I liked my designer products regardless.

Stepping into the kitchen, I froze in my tracks when I spotted Darcie. She was already dressed in a flowy skirt with a shirt that knotted under her breasts, giving a glimpse of her bare stomach.

"Shit," I cursed, taking her in.

"What? Does this not work?" she asked, looking down at her outfit. Paired with her boots and hat, she was a cowboy's wet dream.

"Oh, Sunflower. It fucking works. Too well. I'm going to be fighting off men all night who try to touch what's mine," I growled.

Her eyes widened at my words. I stalked forward, no longer waiting to stake my claim. Pulling her close, a floral scent fell over me as I pressed my lips to hers, searing it into my memory. This would be the last girl I ever kissed.

Drawing back, I took in her rosy cheeks, bright eyes, and plump lips. She stared at me, a little dazed.

"You ready?"

She nodded, taking my hand as I led her out of the room. Cowboy shouted something, but I was too busy forming plans to keep Darcie out of harm's way and not kill anyone.

I decided to take the truck, unsure if I'd be able to control myself if she wrapped her arms around me. I'd be pulling over a mile from here to have my way with her. Opening the passenger side door, I lifted her up, surprising her as she squeaked. Winking, I walked around and got in, not wasting time starting it.

Soft music played as I concentrated on driving, too worried I'd crash if I looked over at her. When she spoke, it was a punishment and reward wrapped in one.

"I didn't expect you to be the way you are."

"How so?" I asked, peeking a glance at her.

"You come off as the flirty fuck boy. I figured you'd be good for a night but wasn't sure there was longevity there."

My hands tightened on the wheel. Her words pierced something in me. For so long, that had been precisely who I was. It was easier to give people what they wanted.

But that wasn't the entire truth. I did it so I wouldn't have to show the real me.

"And now?" I asked, my voice cracking.

"I'm finding out all these layers about you. You're intriguing, kind, passionate, and a good friend. And did I mention sexy? Yep, you're definitely that." She giggled, the sound soothing some broken pieces in me.

"Are you sure you're looking at the right person?" I joked out of habit.

"I can see through your jokes, Laws." Her voice was soft, and the use of the name she'd given me made my heart race.

I took a deep breath, letting it out slowly. "Sorry. It's a reflex. People tend to only want the jokey, playboy version of me."

"I'm sorry you think that's all you have to offer them because you're so much more."

"You're too good for words, Darcie. You have no idea the power you have over me right now."

"Hmm. I can imagine. You're affecting me as well. Whether you believe it or not."

I swallowed, glancing over at her. I wasn't sure what to say after that. We'd both just been vulnerable, dropping our shields. But what did we do next? I decided to take a chance.

"I grew up with an OCD mother. Every aspect of my life was controlled to perfection. Our house was meticulously cleaned, our clothes were the best, and we were always on our best behavior. I didn't realize home was meant to be warm and inviting. I thought the museum I lived in was normal."

"That's why your room is so meticulous?" she asked, turning to look at me.

"Yeah. Some things are harder to stop than others, especially when I like things to be clean. It's hard to separate the knee-jerk reaction to what is healthy."

"How did you get into modeling?"

"My mother. She started me at a young age. It was fun at first. A way to make my mom happy and earn toys. When I got older, I saw it for what it was—another way she controlled what the public saw. It was about her image. Being a Lawson came with expectations, and most weren't enjoyable. When I was able to escape her clutches, I used modeling as a way to support myself. Unfortunately, without my mother there to control my career, I made reckless decisions to exert my freedom, leaving me in vulnerable positions."

"What happened?" she asked.

I shook my head, not ready to go down that road tonight.

"Another time, Sunflower."

"Sorry, I didn't mean to pry."

"No, it's okay. I just don't want to open that can tonight. I want to stay in this moment with you."

She reached over and squeezed my leg. Her touch sent shivers through my body, instantly waking up my cock.

"How did you meet Bubba?"

"He was the one to pull me out of that darkness. I was

here for a photo shoot and was out drinking with some of the other models. We had way too many drinks and ended up at the tattoo parlor. Everyone was daring the other to get something. I ended up in Bubba's chair. I guess he saw something in me. He refused to tattoo me but offered me a place to crash. In doing so, he gave me something I had never had before. A true friend and, eventually, a brother."

"I never would've guessed that by looking at him."

"That's Bubba for you. He's a big softie under all of his muscles and tattoos. With his help, I crawled out of the darkness I'd been trapped in. With his guidance, I was more selective about my modeling jobs, allowing me to stay away from the dark parts and reap the benefits. He taught me how to ride a motorcycle and introduced me to a hidden passion for fixing up cars. He saved my life."

"That's why you're willing to do this relationship? Because of Bubba?"

"Yes and no. Jackson leaving was hard. It shifted something in us all. I honestly thought Cowboy was crazy. I was going to pretend to be okay with the playboy lifestyle as long as I could pull it off. It seemed easier than falling in love and risking losing my family. So, yeah, wanting to stay together is a big draw. But I also believe in it. Together we can love one woman like she deserves to be loved. I've seen it in action, and so have you. I can't argue that it's not worth trying. Can you?"

I pulled into the parking lot of the bar and turned to Darcie. Her eyes searched mine, looking for something.

"No, I can't. I do want this. I just wanted to hear it from you."

My heart settled, my grin returning as I stared at the beautiful girl.

"Then let's boogie, Sunflower. Here's to a night you'll never forget."

Dear Mom,

For the first time since I started writing you, I feel hesitant about telling you something. I don't think you would judge me, but the world has pretty firm beliefs about this sort of thing.

But since this is my journal and my place to process, here it goes.

I have my own harem.

What is that, you ask? Well, when more than one guy likes a girl, and the guys agree to share the same girl, they form a harem.

Doesn't that sound lovely?

I'm going to assume you said yes because it is. It's very lovely.

It's also very hot, and thoughts of what it will be like with multiple partners are filling my mind currently.

But really, it's the best solution for my problem. I like too many people. Maybe it's some weird attachment thing because of the trauma, but I'm going to believe it's because I have a big heart capable of loving more than one person.

So, I am.

Brooks and Grayson are currently on board. I just need to figure out Bubba. I think I have an idea, though. And I feel confident these lips will be kissed soon.

And if Maddox ever returns, we'll figure it out.

I could cry at how relieved that makes me.

I'm trying not to think the worst, that this means something terrible will happen and enjoy the copious amounts of pleasure I will receive instead.

And hopefully, tonight will be the start of that.

Kisses,

Darcie

CHAPTER 12

Darcie

DANCING WITH GRAYSON was a lot of fun. He knew his body well and could move it. The rest of the crowd faded away as we danced. The feel of his arms on me was the only thing I focused on.

"Thank you for bringing me here. I forgot how much I needed to dance."

"You're welcome, Sunflower."

"Why do you call me that?" I asked, curious. The other nicknames had been silly and fun, but this one felt different.

"Because you're like a sunflower for several reasons."

"Oh?" I asked, fluttering my eyelashes. As was his nature, I expected him to tell me a cheesy reason.

"Like the sunflower, you have a strong base and have risen up despite the harshness of the outside world." He twirled me, his eyes raking over me as he stared down. "Sunflowers are made up of a thousand little flowers that form together. Each seed is self-suffi-cient, able to grow wherever it lands. No matter where you go, Darcie, you flourish, leaving your mark on others, much like the pollen of a sunflower." Grayson dipped me, pulling me flush to him. "Sunflowers are also known to have healing properties, and I see you doing that with the three of us guys." His mouth moved toward my ear, his voice softer. "But most of all, you attract the sun, making you reflect pure sunshine. You're casting out the darkness in our lives and replacing it with light."

His voice tickled my neck, and I gasped. Pulling back, I searched his eyes, wondering if it was a line. Spotting the truth, I hid my face in his shoulder as my cheeks turned red.

"You see me a lot differently than I see myself," I admitted.

"Hmm. Then I'll remind you daily until you see it too, Sunflower."

My heart raced; the emotion was overwhelming. I couldn't be falling for him this soon. I'd be a goner if I did.

Grayson rocked us, moving to the rhythm of the song. He hummed in my ear, sending vibrations through me. He stepped back, easily falling into a two-step as he twirled and pulled me closer. We danced together flaw-lessly, our feet in sync. If I didn't know better, I'd think we'd been dancing together for years.

When the song ended, I had a massive smile on my

face. My breathing had increased; my face flushed from the moves. And if I was honest, Grayson.

"Want to grab a drink?" I asked, needing some space. If I kept feeling his body against mine, I'd combust.

"Yeah." Grayson took my hand and led me through the crowd. I caught a few glances from others, but they mostly kept to themselves. It was a welcomed relief.

"Water?" he asked, glancing back at me when we reached the bar.

"Yep." He turned back, placing the order. Two waters were placed on the counter, and he slid some cash across, picking them up. His hand never left mine as he moved us toward an open table.

I sighed when I sat, my feet reminding me I was wearing boots. The price of cuteness was steep when dancing.

Drinking half the bottle, I placed it on the table, feeling better.

"Are you having fun?" Grayson asked, staring at me.

"So much," I said, smiling. I loved the way he stared at me. It made me feel like the only woman around.

"I'm glad. Whenever you need to dance, just let me know."

"I'll hold you to that."

"Good." He smirked, the movement lifting his eyes. They sparkled, making those butterflies in my stomach go crazy.

Feeling out of sorts, I grabbed the water and finished it, hoping it would cool me off in more ways than one.

"You want to dance some more or head out?"

"Dance?" I asked, not ready to quit just yet.

Grayson stood from the stool, offering me a hand. Placing mine in his, I sucked in a breath as my skin erupted in goosebumps.

I could keep fighting my attraction and the feelings accompanying it. Or I could give in and trust that he'd stay.

The way my body leaned toward him, I knew there was no way I'd be able to keep fighting this. Grayson had a pull over me that went straight from his eyes to my clit and to my heart.

The music changed to a sultry song, adding an extra layer of heat as our bodies moved together. Grayson's hand slid down my arm, over my shoulder, as he placed it around his neck. I could feel the path his fingers had taken, marking me with his heat.

It felt like magic was in the air as we swayed together. My hips moved, my feet kept the beat, but my focus was on his face, holding his eyes as the world fell away. His hands moved again, creating more paths of heat in his wake across my back.

Spinning, my hair flew out behind me, the bar a blur as it whirled by. At that moment, he and I were the only two people who mattered.

"Laws?" I whispered, needing something.

"I feel it too, Sunflower."

Nodding, I blinked as I held back tears. The emotions raced through me, overwhelming me as I tried to process them. What was happening between us?

A faster beat started, and we began to move. Our touches were more deliberate as we trailed fingers across one another. The heat built, my breath catching with each twist and turn. When he dropped me, catching me by my neck in a dead drop, I was stunned and turned on.

My body hadn't hesitated to follow him. It seemed I trusted him instinctively.

His fingers flexed before he lifted me up, bringing our bodies together. The blood rushed back, leaving me dizzy. Grayson kept hold of me, offering me his support. We stayed staring at one another, only slightly swaying.

The song ended, and reality returned. But I couldn't ignore how magical the world felt. Grayson did that.

"Want to get out of here?" he asked.

I nodded before he finished. There was no more hiding or debating. All the little touches and heat between us had grown to an inferno, and I couldn't—no, I wouldn't—ignore it.

His hand grasped mine, a smile on his face as he led us out. An uncomfortable feeling washed over me, the hair on the back of my neck standing as we passed through the bar. I looked around, searching for the cause.

Nothing stood out, the feeling eased, and I wondered if I'd just imagined it.

Movement in the corner caught my eyes, a face that shouldn't be there flashing in my mind. I stopped, searching the space, but found it empty.

Grayson turned, his brows raising as he assessed me. "Everything okay?"

"Yeah. I thought I saw someone. But that's not possible. Just my mind playing tricks on me, I suppose."

"You sure?" he asked, stepping closer. His hands went to my shoulders, soothing the anxiety away.

Blinking, I nodded. His presence comforted me, calming my nerves.

His cocksure smile returned, and he bent down, kissing me. "Let's go then."

The rest of the way out of the bar breezed by, the outside air cooling my skin as we headed to the truck. Grayson opened the door, turning and lifting me into it.

"I can climb up," I said, giggling at the motion.

"I know. I just like picking you up. Plus, it's an excuse to put my hands on you."

He stepped forward, and my legs opened to welcome him in. His hands landed on my thighs, squeezing as he neared. At this height, we were eye to eye.

"I shouldn't admit this, but I've fallen hard for you, Sunflower. I want nothing more than to take you back and show you just how much."

"Then do it," I whispered, leaning forward to press our lips together.

He didn't hesitate, wrapping his arms around me and pulling me even closer. My legs wrapped around him, his body flush against mine.

Grayson kissed me, and I forgot my name. His tongue swirled passionately with mine, his arms holding me to him. Grayson kissed with his whole body. It was intense and magical, pulling me further under his spell.

My hips naturally rocked against him, my body responding to the pleasure he was eliciting in me. A pornographic sound left him, his moan vibrating through me as he grunted against my lips.

"Get a room," someone shouted, followed by laughter.

Drawing back, we laughed, my head falling to the space between his neck and shoulder.

"Thanks, we will," Grayson shouted over his shoulder, waving.

Giggling, my body shook as endorphins coursed through me.

Grayson dropped a soft kiss on my forehead and stepped back. Once my feet were secure in the truck, he shut the door and jogged around the front.

Within seconds, he was behind the wheel with his seat belt buckled. The engine started, and he practically bolted out of there, taking a few turns short.

"Careful," I shouted, my smile a permanent fixture in his presence.

He grunted but slowed, his fingers tapping on the wheel as we drove back to the house. The journey felt longer, our constant looks at one another doing nothing to quell the desire between us.

Grayson parked and reached for me, unbuckling my seatbelt before I could. He pulled me to him, carrying me out of the truck as he marched toward the house.

My arms wrapped around his neck, my feet swinging over his arm as he continued on his journey. He had one destination in mind and wasn't stopping until we reached it.

The TV was on when we entered. Grayson ignored the guys watching some show as he moved through the house. I waved over my shoulder, giggling.

"Can't talk, have things to do," he shouted as he neared his room. He stepped into it, throwing his door closed. In a few more feet, I bounced as he tossed me on the bed, his hands moving to unbutton his shirt. I joined him, kicking off my boots and untying mine.

"Fuck," he cursed when I sat there in my bra. "I'm half tempted to tell you to keep the rest on. There's something inherently sexy about you in a skirt."

I smirked, reaching back to unzip it. Slowly, I pulled the material away, leaving me sitting on his bed in only my panties and bra.

Grayson's shirt was off, his hands frozen on the zipper of his pants. My cam girl days came rushing back, so I lifted up on my knees and reached back for my bra. Grayson's chest froze; his breathing halted as he waited for me to undo it.

Unclasping it, I brushed the straps off my shoulders, the cups falling forward to let my breasts spill out. Grayson's breath returned, rushing out in a whoosh. It seemed to speed up his movements as he yanked his pants down, kicking them away, forgetting he still had on his boots. Cursing, he tried to keep his eyes peeled on me as I fell back to the bed, my fingers teasing at the sides of my panties.

Enjoying the attention, I took my time pulling them off, tossing them to him when he seemed to freeze again. The action kick-started him, and he dove for me, somehow managing to get his pants off.

Grayson's mouth found mine, his hands moving over my skin. I lost control of what was happening as his touch heated every part of me. My legs fell to the sides, letting him get closer. I wrapped them around him, wanting to feel him even more.

His lips moved down my neck, zipping tingles through me as he sucked and nipped my skin. My hands threaded through his hair, tugging as he traveled over me.

"I'm crazy for you, Sunflower. I can't decide what I want to do first. You've intoxicated me. I'm drunk on your skin, your smell, your touch..."

Grayson punctuated his words with a kiss as he continued down my body, his hands traveling lower. Finding my opening, he speared me, surprising me as he plunged his digits deep into me. My head fell back, my arms gripping him as I moaned.

"You're so wet for me. That's the hottest thing in the world, Sunflower."

He kept moving his fingers in and out, my pleasure ramping up with each thrust. When he pulled his fingers out completely, I whined. It didn't last long as he sealed his lips to my clit, sucking it as he yanked my thighs up.

I gripped the bedsheets and tried to hold on as the

orgasm rocked through me. It hit me hard and fast, taking my breath away.

My thighs shook against his hold, my body tingling all over. I cried out, my voice breaking as I continued to come hard.

He turned me over, lifting my legs as he positioned himself behind me and rolled on a condom. He paused for a second, leaning over to whisper in my ear.

"I'm going to take you hard and fast the first time. I'm so desperate for you that I can't do it any other way. If you don't want that, now's the time to tell me."

His voice was rough, the need clear in his words.

"Yes. Fuck me hard," I panted, unable to say anything else.

Grayson's hands weaved through my hair, pulling from the roots as he drew my head back to his lips. His other hand gripped my hip, flexing against my flesh.

One second I was empty, needing something to fill me and remove the emptiness; the next, he plunged deep, my mouth forming an 'o' as all thought left me. He held me to him, letting me adjust to his size.

"You're doing great, Sunflower." His hand in my hair soothed my scalp, giving me a momentary reprieve. When I relaxed, he took that as his sign to move.

True to his word, he moved hard and fast, keeping me tight to him. His thrusts were shallow, stretching me as he pistoned in and out. Kissing my cheek, he released my hair and dropped both hands to my hips.

I fell forward, bracing myself on my elbows as he

fulfilled his promise. My toes curled, my entire body tingling as he fucked me hard and deep. I was on the brink of waving the white flag, my body at max capacity for orgasms as his fingers tightened, a grunt falling from his lips as he stilled. A breathy moan spilled from him as he came.

My mind was dazed as I tried to regroup. My body felt like it had been through an intense workout. Muscles I didn't know I had hurt; my body was truly well spent.

Grayson turned me over, pulling me into his arms. He kissed me softly, his hands brushing against my arms.

"We'll clean up in a second; I just want to hold you for now."

I nodded, enjoying his embrace. I sighed happily, relaxing fully in his arms.

"Are you sure that was okay?" he asked. I could hear the hesitation in his voice, making me want to soothe all the doubt away.

"It was perfect, Laws."

His eyes sparkled, and he bent down, kissing me again.

True to his word, a few minutes later, we got up, taking a quick shower to rinse off. I laughed as he played around the whole time, the jokester returning.

I was learning that there were multiple facets of Grayson Lawson, and I was eager to know them all.

Diary #12

Dear Maddox,

It's been a few weeks since I wrote you, and I wanted to let you know that I'm okay. There was a time when I didn't know if I'd ever be again. But I am.

Life has a funny way of reminding you how capable you are.

Knowing I have Chase to thank for my current growth is weird. If he hadn't decided to be an asshole and bombard me at my apartment, I'd still be in Nashville, working at the Saloon and keeping people at arm's length.

Because I did.

No matter how many friends I had, they weren't close to me. They never knew the real me. Only Lennox got close enough, and that's because she's persistent.

Chase set me on a new course, one that has led me to three men who set my soul on fire.

That might be strange to tell you that, but I don't think so.

One, you'll never actually read this. But two, I know you'd be happy for me. You didn't want me to waste my life pining for you. You saw the amount of love I could give someone and encouraged me to go out and find it. That's one of the most amazing gifts you could've given me.

Freedom to explore and love.

I know I shouldn't say I love them yet since it's only been two weeks, but I'm starting to feel that. At least with Grayson and Brooks. I think I was already half in love with Brooks, to begin with.

Bubba continues to be stubborn, holding out on giving in to the attraction between us. I've alternated between the tattoo shop and the garage, but no matter how much time I spend with him, I haven't gotten him to bend. Yet.

He's finally taking me to look at bikes this weekend. I've decided to pull out all the stops and not let him brush me aside any longer. If subtle flirting and teasing aren't enough, then I'll make the first move. I'd like to see him try to get out of the web I'm going to wrap him in.

I left you another message. I hope you find it soon. I miss you always.

Love,
Sensational Darcie

WAKING up next to Grayson and Brooks had become my norm over the past few weeks. Grayson was proving to be insatiable and fucking me in practically every square inch of the house, any chance he got.

Brooks had joined us a few times, proving his penchant for watching translated off the screen into real life. Sometimes he would participate by touching me while Grayson took me from behind, and others, he simply watched while stroking himself. Brooks and Grayson's kinks perfectly balanced one another, making me one very lucky gal.

Though, despite the connection Brooks and I shared, things were moving slower with us physically. But I was okay with it. Brooks was shy in many ways, and I didn't want to overwhelm him until he was ready.

Staring into his eyes now, my hand gripping his cock as Grayson rocked into me from behind, I knew it wouldn't be long until we crossed that line. His fingers brushed against my clit, spreading my wetness as he found the perfect rhythm.

"Yes, yes, yes," I panted, my head rolling back on Grayson's shoulder.

My leg was lifted over his hip as he impaled me from the side. His arms were wrapped around me, holding me close to him. His teeth grazed the area between my neck and collarbone, sending tendrils of pain and pleasure rushing through me.

"Look at how good she takes my cock, Cowboy. I bet you can't wait to be in our girl," Grayson purred, grabbing Brooks' attention.

Over the past few days, Grayson had been amping up his push for Brooks to step outside of himself. It was sweet how he wanted his friend to take the plunge and cross that finish line with me. I couldn't deny I was ready as well.

I whimpered as Brooks' eyes dropped to where he was touching me, his other hand moving to my breast. He licked his lips, his breathing quickening as I stroked him.

"You're so hard, Cowboy. I love feeling you in my hand." I knew how much he liked it when I spoke to him, telling him how he pleased me. His cock jerked in response, his eyes jolting up to my face.

Whimpering again, I beckoned him closer, needing to feel him against me. Grayson thrusted into me harder as I squeezed Brooks. Lunging forward, his hand cupped my cheek as he kissed me sloppily, our mouths hungry for one another.

With a tweak of my nipple and clit, I came so hard I blacked out for a moment as stars filled my vision. My muscles tensed, my whole body trembled as I came with a rush.

Blinking open my eyes, I found Brooks staring at me, a look of reverence on his face. His thumb brushed against my cheek as he watched me.

"I love watching you come. It's so beautiful."

"Why, thanks, bud," Grayson said, chuckling.

Brooks reached over and slapped him, rolling his eyes at his MC brother. Giggling, I cherished the moment of pure happiness as I was held by these two men. I felt safe and secure with them, something I hadn't experienced in a long time.

Sighing, my eyes closed, knowing there were still two pieces missing. One of which was being a complete pain in my ass.

Bubba hadn't fallen for any of my attempts yet. If anything, the closer I grew to Brooks and Grayson, the more he pulled away. When he didn't think I was watching, I could see the yearning in his eyes as he observed us. But he wouldn't talk to either of them about it and ignored me as much as he could.

I was becoming so frustrated with him; I was *this* close to shaving off his beard in his sleep. Maybe then he'd actually talk to me!

At least today, he couldn't get out of spending time

with me. We were headed to look at a motorcycle one of his buddies was selling. It would be the longest time we'd been alone together since that first day.

"How are you feeling about the plan today?" Grayson asked, smoothing my hair back. He kissed me softly, his arms wrapped around me.

I'd learned that after he disposed of the condom, he was a cuddle whore. He would hold me for a while and then take care of me after in the shower, pampering me with soft and delicate touches. It was his way of balancing some of the hardness he tended to show during sex.

Brooks crawled back into bed, pulling the blanket over the three of us. I hadn't noticed he'd gotten up to take care of things. Reaching out for him, I pulled his arm toward me and linked our fingers together. Touching them both like this was everything.

There wasn't anything between them, despite my begging. They were just comfortable enough to share a woman together without it being sexual with one another.

"Sunflower?" Grayson asked, smiling against my cheek.

"Oh, right. Plan. Yes. Ready," I said, sentences not forming just yet.

They both chuckled, the sounds vibrating through my naked body.

"You're so cute when you're dick drunk," Grayson

whispered, kissing me again. The man was affectionate in all ways.

"Hmm, yeah." I nodded, not disagreeing.

Brooks' alarm sounded, so he reached over to turn it off. They were working today in hopes it would force Bubba to surrender to me easier. I wasn't sure who was more at their wit's end, them or me.

"If he doesn't succumb today, what do we do?" I asked, some doubt entering my mind as we headed to the shower.

"Do you honestly think someone can resist you, Darcie?" Brooks asked, lifting his eyebrow.

"Uh, yeah." I rolled my eyes. Boys were so dumb sometimes. "I'm confident in who I am, but I'm also aware that not everyone is attracted to everyone. I can't force him."

"He wants you. He's just stubborn," Grayson added, stepping under the spray.

I trusted them since they knew Bubba better and hoped they were right. No matter how confident you were, a flat-out rejection stung.

Thirty minutes later, I was dressed in a tight pair of jeans with rips on the front, a thin tank top with sequin lips over my breasts, and a leather jacket that Grayson had bought me. Combined with some new boots, I looked every bit the biker chic. Now it was time to see if it worked on Bubba.

Walking into the kitchen, I spotted Bubba at the bar, leaning across it as he drank his coffee. At the sound of my entrance, he glanced up, his eyes going wide before he sprayed the gulp of coffee he drank.

Grayson's hands landed on my shoulder as he bent down to whisper in my ear. "Oh yeah, it's working, Sunflower."

Smiling with a renewed sense of purpose, I swayed my hips more as I grabbed a plate and placed some food on it. Bubba grumbled as he cleaned up the mess, bringing a smile to my lips.

"Something wrong, Waylon?" I asked, fluttering my eyelashes. He froze, turning back to me, his eyes raking over me.

"Nope," he grunted, shifting his body opposite me as he finished cleaning.

"Hmph," Grayson hummed, laughing to himself. Brooks snickered into his coffee cup, enjoying the show.

Smiling, I leaned forward, my cleavage on display as I took a bite. Letting out a breathy moan, I continued to eat my food like it was the best thing ever prepared. Bubba's hands tightened on the counter's edge, his knuckles turning white.

"If you want to go, we need to leave now," he barked, then turned and rushed out of the kitchen.

The guys chuckled, waving me off so I could follow him before he decided to leave me. Stepping outside, Bubba was already in the truck with the engine running. Opening the door, I heaved myself into the massive cab, missing having one of the guys do it for me. Apparently, I'd grown accustomed to being lifted into this thing.

"Your truck's too big," I grumbled as I pulled myself up.

"No, you're just too short," he grunted, his eyes shifting to me. I lay panting across the seat, my feet dangling from the side. I had to be showing a good amount of boob in this position. It was unintentional, but I'd take it.

Growling back at him, I heaved myself the rest of the way, sitting back against the seat.

Bubba didn't say anything, but his ears were red, and he had a smirk on his face.

The drive was quiet, and with each conversation I started, he either ignored or shut me down with a one-word answer. When we pulled into a parking lot, I was ready to get out of the truck and away from the infuriating man.

Jumping down, I didn't wait for him as I strode into the place. Everyone stopped, and I remembered I'd just walked into a biker space alone. The men checked me out, their eyes assessing me from head to toe.

"Howdy. What can we do for you, miss?" a greased-up man asked from the side.

The door opened behind me, and I prayed it was Bubba. This wasn't the day for me to run my mouth and get myself into trouble.

"Ranger," Bubba said, his tone commanding.

A different man than the one who spoke stuck his head out from under the bar, lifting his eyes to meet Bubba's.

"Hey, man," he greeted, placing down the drink he'd been working on. "You here for the bike?"

"Yep. Is it around back?" Bubba asked.

"Yeah. Go ahead and look at it. I'll be there in a second."

Bubba grabbed my shoulder and spun me, pushing me in front of him as he headed back out. I could hear him mumbling something under his breath, but it was too quiet to make out.

Walking around the corner, I spotted the Victory Vegas as I neared. Thoughts of Bubba left me as I crouched down to look at it closer. Whistling, I inspected the parts, running my hand over her. She was once chrome and metallic red, the paint now faded and chipped, but I could see the bike she'd become. I wanted her.

"She's beautiful," I said with awe.

Bubba grunted, but something in the sound was different, making me turn my head to stare at him.

"Not right now, she's not," he started, my hackles rising as he insulted *my* bike. "But she will be," he added, running his hand over the seat, the black seat covered in duct tape.

"Does that mean you approve?" I asked, giddiness flowing through me.

"Hmm," he said, stepping back. "Maybe. I have a few questions."

Ranger walked around the corner, a big smile on his face. He was around mid-thirties with shaggy dark hair and kind eyes. His smile was welcoming as he greeted us.

"Bubba, it's so good to see you. This your sister?" he asked, glancing at me.

Bubba's face turned scarlet, a curse forming on his lips. I knew it had hit a sore point with him, the age difference between us.

"Nope. Girlfriend," I said, reaching my hand out. Bubba choked as Ranger took my hand to shake, surprise covering his face.

"Girlfriend? I'll be. I never thought Bubba would settle down with an old lady."

"As you can tell, there's nothing old about me." I winked, making Ranger laugh.

"How much?" Bubba asked, clearly over the conversation.

"For you, $4000. She needs a new engine, muffler, and exhaust. You'll need to fix her up, but I reckon she'll run real good for you when you're done."

I jumped up and down, clapping my hands. "She's perfect."

Bubba rolled his eyes, the corner of his mouth tilting up despite his attitude. He could deny it all he wanted, but I was growing on him.

I gave Ranger the money Slade had gotten for my car, leaving me with enough money to even buy some cute shoes. With the leftover amount, the money I had saved, and everything I'd earned so far, I still had a nice little nest egg. The guys had been paying me a lot, despite my best efforts to tell them they didn't have to. They'd all given me so much; it felt wrong to take their money for helping out. But they were as stubborn as I was.

Within ten minutes, we had the bike loaded into the back of the truck. I couldn't quit staring at it, knowing soon it would be mine to ride.

Sighing, I broke myself away from it and opened the door. Hands landed on my hips, lifting me into the air. Gasping, my palms landed on his as he placed me on my seat.

"Thanks," I mumbled. My brain had gone haywire from his touch.

He grunted, not responding as he walked around to the other side. The move stunned me speechless, making it difficult for me to find a topic of conversation the whole drive home.

"You okay?" he asked, turning off the truck.

"Me, yeah? Why?" I asked in a rush.

"You're quiet. It's not like you to be quiet."

"Oh, um. Just thinking about my bike," I lied. "Can we start on it now?"

He stared at me, his jaw ticking. "Not today. I need to run to the shop."

"Fine. I'll go with." Smiling at his frown. I knew he was trying to get away from me, but he'd have to be rude to deny me now. Bubba might be stubborn, but he was a gentleman.

"I'm leaving now," he barked, attempting to shake me.

"Okay."

I grinned, showing teeth. "Truck or your bike?"

His eyes searched mine for a beat before he looked at the truck. I felt he'd pick his bike after being locked up in this cage all day.

"Bike."

Nodding, I opened the door and hopped down, heading straight for it. There was no way I'd let him leave me. Taking the helmet I often used, I put it on and waited for him to walk over.

His steps were slow, almost debating if he really wanted to go through with this. Handing him his helmet, I watched as he accepted his fate and placed it on his head.

I felt him tense as I climbed on, a smile spreading at his reaction. Squeezing my arms around him, I ran my hands up his legs before locking them into position. His breath halted, then slowly released.

I never knew torture could be so fun.

When we got onto the open road, I threw my hands up, letting out a shout of glee as he opened it up. Before the turn, I moved my arms back, slowly running them up his thighs again, deliberately brushing against his groin in the process.

I was playing dirty at this point, but I'd had enough. I moved my hands, running them along his body each time we slowed. Bubba was a rigid block of muscle by the time we pulled into the shop. The lot was empty, so I was surprised when he pulled around to the back to park.

He climbed off his bike so quickly I'd worry he had the runs if I hadn't been stroking him the whole ride. He didn't even take off his helmet, just wore it inside.

Chuckling, I took my time and placed my helmet on the handlebars as I followed him into the shop. It was dark; no one else was here this time on a Sunday.

The door to the office slammed, the sound reverberating through the quiet space. Locking the big door behind me, I crept through the darkness, familiar with the layout by now. I placed my ear against the door, listening.

I should probably feel bad, but the time for us to face this had finally come.

With that thought, I pushed open the door to find Bubba sitting in the chair, his elbows on the desk as he took in deep lungfuls. His eyes were closed, a pained look on his bearded face.

"Don't," he growled as I stepped closer.

Ignoring him, I walked to the front of the desk, bracing my hands on the surface as I faced off with him.

"Why do you always push me away?" I asked, my anger leaking through.

His eyes opened, searing me with their heat. He scowled, bringing goosebumps to my skin. This was it. The line I needed to push him over. It was now or never.

"Do you really need to ask yourself that, *little girl*?"

The slur hit, igniting the fire and rage that was ready to be released.

"Yeah, I do. Because if you took a moment to pull

your head out of your ass, you'd see that I'm the furthest thing from a *little girl*. Men have told me what I could be and who I was my whole life. At first, I thought it meant I was special. But I soon learned it was just a way for men to make me weak so they could take whatever they wanted from me. My virtue. My home. My trust. Gone." I slapped the desk, my eyes spitting daggers back at him now.

He swallowed, some of his anger dropping away at my remarks.

"I've had to crawl through fire to become the woman I am today. So, yeah, I might be younger than you, but I'm no fucking little girl. If you opened your eyes long enough to see me for who I am, you'd realize that, *Waylon*."

The heat returned, his eyes sparking at his name. His pupils were blown, blotting out the color.

"You don't need me," he seethed through gritted teeth.

"Blind and delusional." I climbed onto the desk, crawling toward him until I was right in front of him. He sucked in a breath, watching my every move. He didn't back away, though, encouraging that flame in me. Dropping down onto my butt, I knocked his arms off as I hung my legs over the edge, caging him in.

He leaned back, but I gripped his shirt, pulling him toward me. "Kiss me once, Waylon. Kiss me once, and if there's nothing there, I'll leave you alone. But not until you kiss me."

His jaw clenched, his body a stone wall as he stared at me.

Dropping down onto his lap, I wrapped my arms around his neck, rocking on his hard cock pressed against his jeans. His eyes fluttered closed as he bit back a moan.

Nipping his ear, I made one last siren call.

"Kiss. Me. Dammit."

Diary #13

Dear Lennox,
　　Dick. Drunk.
　　Apparently, it's a thing.
　　Look it up.
　　And call me when you're sobered up from yours.
　　Kisses,
　　Darcie

Bubba

HER WORDS SCORCHED MY INSIDES, sending me plummeting over the edge I'd been desperately trying to hold on to.

My restraint broke, and I reared up, grabbing her as I moved. Her back hit the desk as I braced my arms around her, caging her in this time. Her breasts moved up and down as she breathed, her legs tight around my waist.

"Make sure this is what you want, *little girl*. Because once I take this," I said, moving my hand to cup her, "I'm *never* letting you go." I was baiting her, needing to push her to walk away one more time.

She drew up, her eyes firing as she stared me down. Never in my life had a woman infuriated and enticed me so much.

"Don't call me that ever again," she hissed. "I told you once, I'm not a fucking little girl."

"Then what are you?" I challenged, my hand still gripping her pussy tight.

"Your fucking Queen."

Her words struck, smacking me in the chest like a bullet. Because, of course, she was absolutely right. In the month she'd been here, she'd become my entire world despite my attempts to keep her away.

No matter how much I ignored her, she was always there. Her smell, the sound of her voice, the way she giggled. Her shoes clicking on the hardwood, her attempts at cooking. The way she talked with customers and helped everyone around her feel special. Everywhere I turned, I saw reminders of her. From the house to the shop, to even my fucking bike, I couldn't escape her.

And it seemed my avoidance had finally run its course.

"You're right. You're absolutely right, *my Queen*."

I was tired of fighting her and the way I felt around her. I was tired of hearing my brothers please her and having to retreat to my room with an erection that wouldn't go away. But mostly, I was tired of denying myself the happiness she brought me.

Cowboy and Pretty Boy had known all along this was where I'd end up—hanging by my fingernails as I tried to claw my way back to the surface, back to her.

Darcie's face softened, her hand coming up to cup my face. Her fingers were light as they touched my skin, spreading them across my cheek and beard.

"If you think I want you to let me go, then you haven't been paying attention, Waylon. I'm yours."

The sound of my name on her lips was pure ecstasy. No one called me that outside of Brooks. To everyone else, I was Bubba. The big brother who was always there. The dependable one.

Darcie made me feel like a man.

Without questioning it anymore, I sealed my lips to hers as the world exploded around me. Fire and ice ran through my veins as I kissed the woman underneath me. I'd never be the same after this. Nothing and no one would ever compare to her.

Gasping, I pulled back, needing to kiss every inch of her. My beard brushed against her skin, a growl escaping at the thought of it leaving a mark on her perfect skin.

"Yes," she moaned, tilting her head back so I could kiss her neck. Her hips rocked into me, hitting my cock. The way her hands had roamed my body on the drive here had been pure torture. It had taken the last of my restraint not to fuck her up against the bike when I'd parked.

While that idea was tempting, the image of her naked body spread out for me on my beast; I didn't want anyone outside of my brothers to get a glimpse of her. I'd have to make that fantasy a reality at home, while safely stowed away in the garage.

Fuck. I was so doomed if I was already thinking of next time.

The world spun as I lavished kisses on her, pulling off

her jacket and pushing down the straps of her thin shirt. I'd been so worried I'd have to fight all the guys in Ranger's club when she waltzed in there without a care in the world.

"If you ever walk into another club without me like you did today, I'll tan your hide until you can't walk. Understand?" I growled, needing her to listen to me for once.

Her eyes sparkled as she smirked, and I knew whatever she said, it wouldn't be an agreement.

"Promise?" she teased, lighting up an entirely different part of me.

"I've been holding out for weeks, Darcie. I've had to listen to you moan as my brothers fuck you over and over. Do you really want to go head-to-head with me?"

Her smile grew as she dropped her hands to my jeans, unfastening them and reaching for my hard cock. Her hand wrapped around me, her thumb and fingers unable to touch as she gripped my base.

"I'm up for the challenge," she whispered, sliding off the desk and wrapping her lips around my dick.

I was powerless as she sucked me down, taking me further than I'd expected. Her hand stroked me as her mouth sucked, the motion sending me forward as I braced myself on the desk.

My legs trembled, a tingling in my spine as I already felt my orgasm approaching. Unwilling to let her have it right then, I pulled away, a pop sounding as I fell out of her mouth.

"My turn," I growled, my voice rough with need.

Grabbing her, I turned her on the desk, pulling her pants down over her ass. Lifting her knees up, I spread her legs as I centered on my target.

Her pussy gleamed back at me, wet and ready.

"Your pussy is weeping for my cock. But first, I'm going to treat you, my Queen."

Diving in, I licked up her pussy lips, taking in all of her cream. Moaning, I kept her legs apart as I continued to lick and suck, my tongue delving between her folds and then back to her clit. When her legs shook, I gave one more lick before pulling back.

My beard was soaked with her cream, making me harder as I imagined smelling her for hours after. The primal part of me got off on that.

Grabbing a condom, I slipped it on and lined up my cock. Hesitating, I debated if I was too big for her. No matter how badly I wanted to sink in, I'd never want to hurt her.

"Give it to me," she demanded, turning her head to glare at me. "Now."

Her hands gripped the edge of the desk, her cheeks rosy as she waited for me to fill her. Trusting she knew what she could handle, I pushed forward, her warm pussy lips spreading wide to accommodate me.

"Shit, fuck," I cursed as I felt her tighten around me. Her pussy was like a vise gripping my cock.

"More," she encouraged, pushing her hips back onto

me. I slipped in even further, my legs shaking as I tried to regain control.

Her whimper spurred me into action, not wanting to hurt or disappoint her.

Keeping a hold of her thighs, I pulled her back as I thrust forward over and over. The desk squeaked from the movement; the sound joining our moans as we rushed to find our release.

"Yes, yes, yes," she screamed, her body shaking, her walls tightening around me as she came. It was all it took for my orgasm to push me over the edge. I'd denied my body for so long that it was ready to combust when it finally had her.

Shaking, I held her to me as I came so hard I felt all the cum drain from my balls. She'd literally wrung me dry.

Darcie collapsed onto the desk once I pulled out, panting as she gathered her breath. Once blood returned to my brain, I walked to the bathroom and disposed of the condom. Taking a few wet cloths, I returned to her, gently cleaning her up as she lay there. Once I was done, I wrapped her in my arms, cradling her to my chest. Brushing her hair back, I stared into the eyes of the woman who fit me so completely.

"How are you, my Queen?"

"Good. So good," she mumbled, a soft smile on her lips.

"I'm sorry I've been such an asshole," I whispered,

finding it easier to admit the truth now that it was out in the open.

"It's okay. I kind of like it. It's fun."

"You do know how to press my buttons." I paused, needing to know something. "I'm assuming the guys told you about what our club wants."

"Mm-hmm. Yep. I'm all good. I love all you fuckers," she whispered, her eyes falling closed.

I froze, wondering if she meant that the way it sounded. Sitting back in the chair, I let her sleep for a while as I thought about what this meant.

Pulling out my phone, I opened the group message with my brothers.

Me: I hate you assholes

It didn't take long for them to respond.

PB: Does that mean our little firecracker succeeded?

CB: He's a stronger man than we give him credit for if she didn't.

PB: Nah, he so gave in. My dick radar is going off. Bubba got some.

CB: I don't think that sounds as cool as you think it does, bro.

PB: You're just jealous your dick can't do it.

CB: Again, not something I'd brag about. Weird flex, bro.

Chuckling, I couldn't help but laugh at the two idiots who'd become my family.

Me: Cowboy is right, PB. It's weird. Don't talk about your dick with us.

PB: Is it because mine's the prettiest?

Me: Doubtful.

PB: Want a contest? Sunflower can judge.

CB: I'm still waiting to hear if he gave in to our girl or not first.

Me: She smells of sunshine and honeysuckle.

It was quiet for a few before the phone blew up as multiple texts came through.

PB: Yes! Our brotherhood has a Queen.

PB: How is she? Did she survive?

PB: Who gave in first?

PB: I need the details.

CB: How's Darcie?

Lifting the camera, I took a picture of her sleeping in my arms, her face serene.

Me: *pic attached*

Me: We'll be back soon. I don't want to wake her yet.

PB: God, she's so fucking gorgeous.

CB: She looks peaceful. I guess that means, good job?

Me: You can ask her yourself. I'm not gossiping.

PB: You're no fun. Hurry back.

CB: I'm happy for you, Waylon.

Me: Thanks, brothers. Sorry, it took me so long to believe.

Putting my phone back, I bent down, dropping a kiss on her forehead. Darcie stirred, and my whole world shifted, aligning with her as my center. I meant what I'd said to her. Once I had a taste, there would be no way I could walk away.

She was it for me. Whoever was chasing her just gained three protectors that they'd have to go through first.

Diary #14

Dear Dad,

I got a new bike the other day. It needs to be fixed up, but I can see the beautiful beast she'll be when it's done. I feel alive again in a way I haven't felt since I left Mississippi.

I'm not as angry anymore. Mostly, just sad.

I'm sad that there wasn't another way for us to continue. I'm sad I had to leave my whole life and family behind. But mostly, I'm sad that you haven't gotten to be part of my life.

I hate the control Agonizer has and how he can get away with his shit.

I knew I had to run in the beginning because I was young and unprepared to lead. I needed these years to grow into myself as a person and believe in my strength.

And I do now. I'm strong and fierce, just like you taught me to be.

Recently, my life has grown to include three men. I doubt any father around wants to hear about their daughter and three men, but too bad. The price you pay for making me leave, I suppose.

They make me happy. They make me feel safe and show me how strong I've become.

But mainly, they've shown me love.

I'm tired of running. I'm tired of men like Agonizer deciding my fate.

Maybe it's time to push back.

I'm not ready to risk what I have yet, but I know there will come a day when I have to. And I hope you're there to see it.

Love,
Darcie

CHAPTER 15

Darcie

I TOSSED my bag into the back of the truck, turning to find the guys watching. I smiled, pure happiness radiating out of me. Brooks was taking me with him to the rodeo. I was excited to see him in action and for some alone time without the others.

Since Bubba gave in to me and his feelings, he'd been a different man. He was affectionate and possessive, channeling all the anger and avoidance he had into more productive forms of communication. Such as, whenever I was in his sight, he would pull me into him or cup his hand to my leg, neck, or hip, making it known I was his.

It was a heady and exhilarating feeling.

Between the three of them, I rarely sat in my own seat anymore since they would pull me into their laps whenever I was near. The more they touched and cherished me, the easier I fell head over heels in love with the three men.

"You won't let her out of your sight," Bubba demanded, not making it a question.

"I'm not going to. She's going to sit with a trusted friend while I'm riding. Otherwise, she'll be right by my side. I promise."

Bubba grunted, rubbing his beard as he thought. "I want regular check-ins."

Rolling my eyes, I walked forward, pulling on his shirt for him to lean down. "We'll be fine. We've gone over my self-defense training from the Mavericks, and added some of your Bubba moves. If anyone tries anything, I'll take them down."

I snickered, making his face soften. Every night, we'd been training and reinforcing the things I'd learned all those years ago, along with some dirty fighting moves Bubba wanted me to know. It had gone a long way in helping me feel stronger and regaining control over my fear.

Kissing Bubba, I let go of his shirt as he growled, pulling me back to him. He wasn't going to let me go until he was satisfied. Giggling, I stepped back when he was done, my cheeks already flushed. Bubba lifted his eyebrow, a satisfied look on his face.

Grayson pulled me into his arms before Brooks could claim me again. Giving me a passionate kiss, he spun me back out into Brooks' arms.

"Send dirty pics," Grayson teased, winking as he pulled Bubba to go into the house.

Chuckling, I followed Brooks to the truck and

climbed in. It was quiet as we got onto the highway, large trucks passing by as we merged.

"You excited?" I asked, unable to let the silence go on for too long.

"Yeah. It's been a while since I had a spectator." He glanced over at me, his face full of warmth.

"I've never been to a rodeo before," I admitted. "What's the best part?" I turned a little in my seat, resting my arms on the console so I could watch him easier as he talked.

Brooks' face changed as he talked about the horses, the riders, and the different events. It was a whole new side of him that I was excited about witnessing.

"I hope I'm asking this the right way," I hedged. "How come you're not shy about rodeo? Seems like something you wouldn't want to do? Be in the spotlight?"

"I don't mind being in the spotlight. It's just girls I'm shy around," he said, his cheeks red at the admittance.

"Do you still feel shy around me?" I asked, curious.

He nodded, turning his head for a second to glance at me. "Oh yeah. Though, there's also this confidence I have with you that I've never felt before. I think that the time we spent together beforehand helped me develop a foundation. I'm nervous, but it's not the same intensity."

"I'm glad. I don't want to make you nervous."

"It's only in the best way, Darcie. I'm nervous because of how much I care for you. I don't want to mess up."

"Then trust that I'll tell you if you do and help you figure out the rest."

He grinned, nodding. "Okay."

We listened to music for the rest of the trip, singing along to the ones we knew. He told me stories about him and the guys, making me laugh at some of the crazy things Grayson had done.

"Oh, I can't wait to rib him about that." I laughed, my sides hurting from the movement.

"You didn't hear it from me," Brooks said, turning off the road onto a dirt and gravel one. "We're here."

I sat up and looked out the window, taking in all the horse trailers. The area was filled with vehicles with a large coliseum in the distance.

After we parked, Brooks took my hand and led me to one of the trailers. His ears were still red, but he had a massive smile on his face. Knocking, he stepped back, squeezing my hand.

A man rivaling Bubba's size opened the door, grinning wide as he stepped down and embraced Brooks.

"Langston! You made it."

"Hey, Chief. Can you put me down? I didn't drive all the way here for my girlfriend to see me fall flat on my ass."

"Girlfriend?" he asked, placing Brooks back on his feet. He turned, spotting me as his eyes lit up at my presence. He moved to give me the same type of hug when an arm slapped his chest, halting him.

"Don't you dare, you big oaf," a woman said, stepping out of the trailer.

"Brooks, how are you?" she said, stepping in and giving him a hug. "And girlfriend? Why, aren't you a pretty little thing?" she said, giving me a welcoming smile.

"Hi," I said, waving.

"I'm Kendra, and this is Dave, though most people call him Chief." The big man wrapped an arm around Kendra, dwarfing her. He stared down as she spoke, love and adoration shining from his eyes.

"It's a pleasure to meet you both. I'm Darcie."

"The pleasure is all ours, Darcie. We're just so happy Brooks has found someone. Lord knows I tried for years. But he was waiting for that special someone."

She smiled kindly at Brooks, his cheeks heating more. He looked at me, smiling, though, making me feel loved.

"Darcie is as special as they get," he said, staring at me. This time, it was my cheeks that were blushing.

"Aren't you two the cutest things?" Kendra cooed. "Come in and have some grub before your ride, Brooks."

We spent the next hour in their trailer as Chief and Kendra shared stories of Brooks riding. It was nice getting to hear about him from others.

"Can Darcie sit with you, Kendra, during my heat?"

"Of course, darling. I'll take good care of her."

The guys left soon after, needing to change and get ready. Kendra gave me a tour of the grounds, pointing out the various events that went on.

"Wow, I never realized there were so many different things."

"It's a whole way of life, the rodeo. People here live and breathe it. It's a family, in a way."

I felt her eyes on me, and I had an inclination to what she was getting at.

"Brooks is one of the best people I've ever met. I'm glad he's had people like you to look out for him."

She hummed but dropped it, and I hoped it meant I had passed her inspection.

We grabbed some popcorn and drinks before taking our seats in the stands. A loud horn blared before a gate opened, a horse rushing out as the rider held their arm up, trying to stay on. He didn't last long, falling to the ground in four seconds.

"Ouch," Kendra grimaced as she watched him limp off.

The following few riders lasted a little longer, but no one managed to stay on for eight seconds. When another rider entered the gate, Kendra sat up, tapping my leg.

"Here we go. Now the real competition starts. This guy right here is your boy's biggest threat to winning tonight."

I turned, taking in the man and sizing him up. When the horn sounded, I could instantly spot the difference from the other riders. He was confident and sure, keeping his arm high as he rode the bucking horse. He wasn't fighting it but moving with the creature instead.

The crowd roared when the buzzer went off as he hopped down and sprinted away.

Kendra waited for a score to flash up before nodding, mumbling to herself. "Brooks still has a chance. He's a lot cleaner."

I nodded in agreement, clueless about what she was talking about. After a few more, it was Brooks' turn. The crowd quieted, all eyes on the box as they watched for it to lift. I held my hands together, my heart racing as I waited for the horn to sound.

When it did, the world felt like it was in slow motion as the gate rose and the horse flew out. Brooks was smooth as he rode, his body mimicking the horse's movement as he held on. As soon as the eight seconds were up, the crowd roared when he dismounted, waving as he skipped out of the way. When he spotted me, he ran, hopping up on the fence and tossing me his hat. I caught it as the crowd cheered, my face flaming from the action.

He winked before heading back through a gate and out of sight.

"The boy's clearly smitten. He basically proposed in cowboy speak," Kendra said, her eyebrows lifted as she smiled at me.

Blushing even harder, I placed his hat on my head so I wouldn't lose it. There were only a few more riders to go before the announcer came out and gave out the buckles. I held my breath again as I waited to see if Brooks would win.

"First place goes to Brooks Langston by a tenth of a point!"

The crowd cheered; Kendra turned to me with a huge grin, grabbing my hands as we both jumped up and down. It was a rush, and I could understand why Brooks enjoyed it so much. Even if it did scare the shit out of me to watch him do it.

"Go get your man, honey!" she hollered, pushing me off toward the end of the stands.

I didn't hesitate, rushing toward him, eager to kiss and feel his body close to mine. Hopping off the stands, I walked behind them as I searched for an opening. I wasn't paying attention, so consumed with finding a way to Brooks that I ran smack dab into someone.

"Ouch!" a manly voice shouted as our bodies collided. Hands grabbed me as we fell, stopping me from smacking into the concrete.

"Sorry there, Darlin. I didn't see ya," the smooth voice said. Glancing up, I froze as I stared at Stefan, the wannabe rock star who'd been a horrible bed partner. He smiled down at me, oozing charm as he checked me out. I hadn't thought of him since that awful night when he fucked me and then had his brother, Damon, drive me home.

I didn't want to think of Damon after our last encounter, where he called me names and blew me off when I said I wouldn't commit to just him. A sour pit formed in my belly as I tried to find an escape.

Thankfully, it didn't appear Stefan remembered me

as he continued to steady me as he checked me out. I'd be offended if it didn't mean it was easier now to get away from him.

"Apologies, but my boyfriend is waiting," I said, keeping my voice low. I tugged my arm free, his fingers feeling slimy on me.

His face changed, something sinister appearing in his eyes. "Boyfriend, huh? Well, how do you feel about upgrading to a rock star?" he started, smirking at me. It was so unattractive I wondered what I ever saw in him in the first place.

He was for healing, I reminded myself, not wanting to play the slut shame game now.

"Nah, she's got a rodeo star," Brooks said, coming up and wrapping his arm possessively around me.

I sighed in relief at his touch, my smile forced as I stepped away. Stefan continued to watch us, his gaze appraising as we disappeared. I hoped he hadn't been able to pinpoint who I was. Because I didn't need Damon, or anyone from my life back in Nashville, to know my whereabouts. I'd need to be more careful in the future. Stupidly, I'd let the happiness of meeting the guys diminish my fear.

But the truth was, the bad guys were still out there and looking for me.

"Who was that?" Brooks asked once we'd cleared the area.

"A bad decision," I grumbled. "He served a purpose, but that's about it."

He frowned, my gut tensing. Shit, was he going to break up with me because of this?

"Do you think he followed you somehow?" he asked, turning toward me, his eyes full of concern.

I stopped, my mouth opening. Wrapping my arms around him, I held him to me, remembering my need to feel him earlier. My heart calmed the longer I stood there, his hands brushing up against my back.

"Thank you for being you," I whispered.

"Always." He kissed my forehead, his arms rubbing up and down mine. I took a deep breath as we continued walking. I spotted a sign and pointed.

"I'm guessing that's why he's here. Looks like he's gone solo." I cringed at the image, visions of his pump and dump replaying in my head. My body shuddered at the recall.

"I know we planned to go to the party and stay the night, but what if we just headed home?" Brooks asked.

"Are you sure? You don't have to do that for me."

"I'm sure. I'd rather spend the night with you," he said, his voice growing husky.

Parts of my body woke up, eager to move forward with Brooks.

"Oh?" I asked, trailing my fingers up his shirt. "Is my shy cowboy ready to be tamed?"

His pupils dilated at my words, his throat bobbing as he swallowed. "Yes," he whispered, the sound seductive.

Taking his hand, we both ran as we headed to his truck, laughing the whole way.

THE TENSION WAS THICK AS WE PULLED INTO the driveway. The last hour had been quiet, both of us stuck in our heads. I felt nervous as butterflies erupted in my belly. What if I wasn't what he imagined? What if the cam-version of me was better than the real one?

I turned and looked at him; my nerves turned to goo as I stared at his beautiful face. He smiled, ridding me of all my fear.

"You ready?" he asked, holding his hand out.

Placing mine in his, he pulled me across the seat, placing his arm under my butt to lift me. Giggling, I wrapped my arms around his neck, so enamored with this sweet man.

The house was quiet as we entered. It was around midnight, and neither guy expected us back until morning. Brooks made his way through the house, his eyes focusing on me the whole way.

A switch flipped in him the second we stepped into his room. Brooks' face became determined as he sat me down on the bed.

"I've imagined this so many times; I can't believe it's really happening," he whispered. His hands brushed over my shoulders, pushing my straps down. I'd learned that Brooks had a thing for undressing me. So, I sat back and let him, loving the gentle touches he gave me in the process.

His calloused hands ran down my arms, lifting them to remove my shirt. Slowly and with great care, he pulled it off, placing it on the chair. Next, he unbuttoned my jeans, sucking in a breath when he saw my underwear.

I'd worn the pair he'd sent me. Red crotchless lace with a heart cutout in the back. His hands smoothed over the material, trembling slightly when he moved down to pull off my jeans.

"You're almost too much to bear, Darcie," he said with a pained voice.

Kissing his cheek, I cupped his jaw, bringing his attention back to me.

"I'm all yours, Cowboy. You don't have to be scared."

His eyes closed, nodding as he stepped back to take me in. Unbuttoning his shirt, his eyes never left me as he worked on his buttons. I leaned back on my elbows, crossing my legs as I watched, giving him a proper pose.

Once his shirt was gone, he wasted no time removing his belt, his new buckle gleaming as he undid it and placed it on the table. His boxers were tight as he lowered his jeans, the black fabric stretching to keep his cock contained.

Reaching back, I unhooked my bra, letting it fall. Holding it out to him, I let him take it from my fingers, his eyes glued to my breasts.

Moving my hands to them, I smoothed my palms

across my nipples, fondling each one as I pushed my breasts together, feeling their weight in my palms. Brooks was frozen to the spot as he watched, his eyes never leaving me.

"Your turn," I said, scooting back on the bed. I crooked my finger, beckoning him toward me.

He stepped closer to the bed, bending his knee to crawl closer to me. I took in his magnificent body, my eyes trailing over his abs and the trail of dark hair.

I pushed him back on the bed when he was close, straddling his waist. Reaching down, I stroked my hand over his boxers, his eyes fluttering closed.

"You're sure you're ready?" I asked, needing to hear it again.

His eyes opened, nodding at me. "Yes, Darcie. I'm ready." His hands cupped my face, pulling my lips to his. Brooks kissed like he had all the time in the world, savoring every little nip and touch. Breathless, I pulled back, my head a little fuzzy.

Grabbing a condom, I pulled his boxers down and tossed them on the floor. His cock sprang free, eager to greet me. Brooks hissed as I rolled on the condom, his hands going to the bed as he gripped the covers.

Placing my knees on either side, I lowered myself as I lined up with him. Very slowly, I sank down, feeling him stretch my walls.

Brooks cursed, a moan leaving him as I moved, and I hoped he'd be okay. I didn't want to kill the man the first time I was with him.

"You okay?" I asked, placing my hands on his chest to balance.

He lifted his own to grasp mine, his eyes open. "So good," he whispered, his voice husky and full of need.

Slowly, I rocked forward, moving my hips as I rode him. His hands moved to my hips, lightly tracing the silk as he held me.

"Fucking hell, Rose. I can't believe this is real."

"It's very real, Cowboy." I moved faster, picking up some speed as I adjusted to his size. His eyes rolled back, a moan leaving him.

"I never was able to dream this good," he said, grabbing my hips and helping me grind down harder on his pelvic bone. It hit my clit just right, sending tiny tendrils through me as I rode him.

"Yes, yes," I said, throwing my head back. My hair brushed against my back, tickling my sensitive skin.

Brooks rose up, turning us suddenly as he caged me against the bed. His hands cupped my face as he kissed me, his hips moving forward.

Drawing back, I stared into his eyes, seeing nothing but love shining back. Wrapping my legs around his waist, I moved with him as he pushed me into the bed.

Running my hands down his back, I pulled him to me, pressing his chest into my breasts. His hot breath fanned over my neck as he panted, placing soft kisses there.

Moving one hand between us, I rubbed my clit as he rocked harder, his cock hitting me deeply.

"Yes," I murmured, my orgasm building. It was a soft rolling one that suddenly appeared, crashing through my body in small waves. It lingered, tiny sensations prickling over my skin as my muscles trembled.

Brooks stilled, a long moan leaving him as he stared into my eyes, his body shaking. Pulling him to me again, I held him as he came, his muscles tense.

When we recovered, he pulled back, staring into my eyes.

"I love you," he whispered, kissing gently on my lips. Tears welled in my eyes at the softness of it.

"I love you, too."

Clinging to one another, we made love a few more times between our desperate kisses before we finally passed out.

Dear Mom,

It's hard to believe I've been here a little over a month now. Outside my first day with the creepy guy and the weird run-in with Stefan, I haven't encountered any danger. I'm beginning to believe I fabricated it all.

There's still no word from Maddox, and I can't find anything about his sister. She doesn't seem to exist. I hope that means Maddox was successful and not that his father had her removed from this world.

Dad continues to ignore my attempts to reach out. I'm leaning more toward forgiveness, but it still hurts. I lost so much that I'm not sure I can ever get it back.

Though it doesn't feel like I've lost anything

when I stare across the table at the three men who've captured my heart.

I feel so loved and cherished. Lennox is sick of my sappy letters to her, but it's all her fault, so she has to endure it.

I know I should be worried. The future is still out there, and I have people after me.

It's just hard to care when I'm this blissfully happy.

A few orgasms a day probably helps with that.

My bike is finally ready, and I get to drive it to the shop tomorrow. I'm so excited; it's been too long since I had my own wheels.

I'm looking forward to the freedom and spark of life that motorcycles give me.

I'm still trying to figure out how I can convince Bubba to let me race him there. I'm sure I'll figure something out.

Love,

Darcie

CHAPTER 16

Darcie

SITTING ON BUBBA'S LAP, I ran my fingers through his beard as he worked. His eyes were laser-focused on me, making my heart skip a beat. It was a slow day at the shop, and I was helping him with some paper-work. But so far, all we'd managed to do was spread the papers out on the desk and open the program.

"You know, I've heard how you found the guys and invited them into the Brotherhood, but how did you get it started in the first place?"

My hands ran over his smooth head, his eyes closing. One hand was wrapped around my waist, the other covering my thigh. He opened his eyes when I stopped moving my hands, assessing me.

"You really want to know?" he asked.

Nodding, I smiled. "Yeah, I do."

"The guys told you about Jackson?"

"A little. They mentioned that his leaving was what made you all want to share."

"Yeah." He swallowed, his eyes a little sad.

"If you don't want to talk about it, you don't have to," I hedged. I hadn't meant to pry, but it seemed I'd opened an old scab.

"It's okay. It doesn't hurt anymore. Just makes me sad. He was my best friend for the longest time."

I nodded, laying my head on his chest, hoping it was easier to talk if I wasn't staring directly at him. Bubba shifted down, his legs spreading a little wider under the desk. He took a deep breath, my body moving with the action as he exhaled.

"Jackson and I grew up together. Our ma's were best friends. He came to live with us when his mom died in a car wreck. Our friendship grew into that of brothers, and we were inseparable. I feel bad for Ma for having to deal with all the shit we pulled." He chuckled, the sound low and deep.

"He was the one who got me into motorcycles. His dad wasn't around much, but had left him an old beat-up Honda. The year we turned eighteen, he saved every penny that summer to fix it up. Once we had the bike running, I knew I needed one too. Mostly just so I wasn't left behind. One night, over a bottle of cheap beer, we made a pact to always be brothers in every sense of the word. We'd seen a few older guys at the bars with their leathers and patches, and we figured we'd make our own. That was the night the Brotherhood was born."

I rubbed his chest, not wanting to interrupt his story. Bubba had a dark, smooth voice when he was telling a story, and I enjoyed just listening to him.

"We didn't like the initiation process some of the other clubs had, so we decided ours would be based on a man's character. We got our own patches and leather, made our symbol, and promised to always put the Brotherhood first. A few guys around town were interested in it for a while, but they'd fade out after a few months when it was no longer fun. When I met Grayson, I had a gut feeling he was the type of man we'd been looking for. The same with Brooks. They were like Jackson and me in many ways, looking for something to belong to that mattered, and the Brotherhood gave them that. We might not be the richest or most dangerous club, but that wasn't what it was about for us."

His voice trailed off, the emotion thick. I ran my hand over his chest, hoping to smooth some emotion away with my touch.

"What was it about, then?" I asked.

His eyes dropped down to me, softening around the edges. "Family. We found a family in each other, a brotherhood we could count on. Together, it seemed like we could do anything. I never expected a woman to be the thing that tore us apart. It was why, when he left, I was desperate enough to consider Brooks' insane idea. I didn't want to endure the pain again of losing one of them. I'd get over my jealousy of watching them with my woman if it meant they were in my life."

"Did you tell him you didn't want him to leave?" I asked, curious how his best friend, his brother, could walk away.

"I wanted him to be happy. Mandy made him happy. I've never begrudged him for choosing to start a different life."

"Do you see Jackson or talk to him much?"

He nodded, pushing my hair back. "Yeah. We still talk about once a week. I haven't seen him and Mandy that much since they moved away. They even have two rugrats now. We'll have to take a ride this fall and go visit. They'll love you."

"I'd like that." I smiled, the thought of a future with these men warming my heart. Bubba leaned down and kissed my lips, his beard tickling me.

"Do you get jealous?" I asked, curious.

"Not how you're thinking. It surprised me how happy I was to see you loved and cherished. I was only envious I wasn't the one to do it."

"And now?" I asked, licking my lips.

His answer came in the form of his blowing raspberries on my neck.

Giggling, I pulled back, smoothing my hands over his face. A knock at the door stopped the words that wanted to spill out.

"Yes?" Bubba grunted, shifting so we were sitting up more.

The door opened, and Clive, one of the newer tattoo

artists, stepped in. "There's a man here to see you," he said.

"Tell him I'll be there in a second," Bubba said, sighing.

"No. He's here for Darcie."

Bubba growled, making me laugh. I patted his cheek. "It will be alright, Bubba Bear. It's not like you're going to let me walk up there on my own," I teased.

He smirked, barely letting go so I could stand. Clive watched us, stepping out of the way as we neared. All the employees were happy for Bubba when they saw us together. They all loved and adored him here, telling me how special he was. It had been unnecessary since I already knew it. It was still sweet, nonetheless, to see how much they cared about his happiness.

Bubba trailed a centimeter behind me, barely giving me room to walk. Chuckling at his overbearingness, I pushed him aside as I turned to see who was there for me.

My breath stopped as my heart raced at the sight. The world wanted to spin around me until I remembered to breathe. Taking a step, I was soon running toward the figure.

Their eyes locked on me, watching every move I made as I neared. I could hear Bubba shouting at me, but nothing would stop me from going to this man.

Without thinking, I jumped into his arms, my legs wrapping around him. His arms held me securely to his chest, a hand on my head as his lips fell into my neck.

Tears streamed down my face uncontrolled as I held on for dear life.

"You're here. You're here," I murmured over and over.

"I am, Princess, I am."

His hand rubbed up and down my back, my tears slowing. I pulled back, bracing my hands on his face, looking him over.

Maddox King looked older than when I last saw him. His eyes were darker with shadows, and I wondered what he'd been through. I kept touching his face, his hair, wherever I could reach, just to make sure he was real.

He chuckled, the sound soothing my heart. "I'm real, Princess." His eyes shifted over my head, and I had a feeling whom he was seeing. "I think your bodyguard wants to kill me for touching you," he whispered, smiling.

Exhaling, I tapped his arm to put me down. The urge to kiss him was strong, but this wasn't the place. Nor did I know if he still wanted me that way. Landing on my feet, I turned, taking his hand and leading him over to where Bubba was scowling against a wall.

"Waylon, this is Maddox." I lifted my eyes, trying to communicate now was not the time to cause a scene.

Maddox stretched his hand out to Bubba, offering an olive branch. "It's nice to meet you, man."

Bubba glared down at the offering, his possessiveness coming out to play. Stepping away from Maddox, I wrapped my arm around Bubba and squeezed.

"Play nice. I'll explain."

Bubba grunted, raising his hand to shake with Maddox's. Now that was settled, I knew we had a lot of talking to do, and the shop was not the right place.

"Waylon, can we take lunch now and head over to the garage? There are some things I think everyone should hear."

Bubba glanced down at me, his eyes moving over my face. After what felt like a lifetime, he nodded. "Yeah. Let me tell the guys."

He stepped away, then turned, pulling me to him. Bubba kissed me hard, leaving me slightly breathless as he stomped back to the office.

Maddox coughed, a laugh wanting to spill out. Looking at him, I crossed my arms.

"What?" I asked, daring him to say something since he'd been gone for a few years.

"Nothing. Just seems I make the big guy nervous." He lifted an eyebrow, clearly enjoying the showdown too much.

Rolling my eyes, I grabbed my bag from the front desk as Bubba returned.

"Want to ride with me, Princess?" Maddox asked, probably to ruffle more of Bubba's feathers. Bubba snorted this time, a smile appearing on his face, knowing what I would say.

"Nope." I grinned, reaching in and grabbing my keys. "But you can ride bitch with me."

Bubba chuckled, heading toward the door and

opening it as I approached. Maddox stood stunned for only a second before spinning on his dirty motorcycle boots and heading toward me. He wore a huge smile that I couldn't help but return.

He'd understand what it meant for me to have my own bike again more than anyone.

"Lead the way, Princess," he said right before Bubba let go of the door in his face. Snorting, I shook my head. I shouldn't be enjoying their little digs at one another so much, but I was.

Maddox laughed, shaking it off, and headed toward his bike. I stopped, staring at the Harley Davidson Low Rider, needing to appreciate the beast's beauty. It had been a while since I'd seen the bike, nostalgia coming to the surface as I smoothed my hand over the leather seat. Even Bubba stopped to give it an appreciative nod. They might not like one another, but you didn't disrespect another man's wheels.

The drive to the garage was quick, the three of us riding together, with me at the helm. It felt more natural than I wanted to admit leading them. The thought of Brooks and Cowboy joining our lineup made my skin tingle in anticipation.

Now that would be a sexy image. Me on my bike, leading four hot-ass men on motorcycles behind me.

Oh yeah. That needed to happen. And then a group orgy at the end.

Wait. What? I was getting ahead of myself. I wasn't sure where Maddox stood or if he was even back for good. He had his own missions he was working on, and I wouldn't stand in his way. It wasn't how we worked.

Pulling around to the back of the garage, I soaked in the sound of our bikes together as we parked, my pussy throbbing in response. Seriously, I might have a problem. Probably just inhaled too many exhaust fumes. Yeah, that had to be it.

Brooks immediately came out of the garage, a smile on his face as he wiped his hands. He didn't hesitate as I stepped closer to wrap me in his arms and kiss me. And as had become custom, as soon as he was done, Grayson twirled me into his, giving me his greeting.

Breathless and more turned on, I glanced back at Maddox, wondering what he thought. Surprisingly, he only watched me with a curious expression. There was no disgust or judgment at all in his expression.

"Brooks, Grayson, this is Maddox, my dearest and oldest friend."

Brooks' eyes shot to mine, happiness filling his eyes at the name. He was the first to step forward, offering his hand.

"Hey, I'm Brooks. Darcie has told me a lot about you. I'm glad you found her."

"Nice to meet you, Brooks."

Grayson stood back, assessing Maddox, glancing at Bubba to gauge his response.

He stepped forward, keeping an arm around me as he shook Maddox's hand.

"So, what's the occasion?" he asked, looking at me.

"I figured we should all talk, and it was easier to do it here. Is your office free?"

Grayson searched my eyes before nodding. "Sure thang, Sunflower. Lead the way."

We all gathered in the office, taking up positions. Bubba leaned against the door, and Maddox took a chair, that shit-eating grin still on his face letting me know he found this whole situation hilarious. Brooks sat next to Maddox in the other chair, and Grayson pulled me with him to the one behind the desk.

Everyone was quiet, and I realized they were waiting for me. Taking a deep breath, I turned to Maddox.

"There's a lot that's happened since you left. But to bring you up to date, Agonizer is looking for me; I might've killed Chase, and I'm in a relationship with these three men."

Maddox's smile dropped as he shifted forward, his face changing to one of concern and perhaps a little fear. I didn't know which part worried him—the three men I was dating or our past.

"I'm glad I got here when I did then. It seems we have a lot to discuss."

Nodding, I sat back, needing Grayson's arms to comfort me and show Maddox I trusted these three with everything.

"Start at the beginning. What happened once you left me in Nashville?"

Maddox nodded, his eyes piercing mine as he filled in the blanks.

Diary #16

Dear Mom,

~~Things are about to get interesting.~~

~~The other shoe has dropped.~~

~~The shit has finally hit the fan.~~

Screw it. I've got nothing.

Love,
Darcie

CHAPTER 17

Maddox

SIGHING, I took a deep breath as I stared around at the men Darcie had gathered around her. My pride wanted to rage at these men believing they could replace me. But my heart had always known Darcie was a woman worthy of lots of love. If she chose these men to be by her side, then I'd trust they were worthy of her.

It didn't mean I would lie down and roll over, though. It wasn't in my nature to give up. I'd fight to have a place along with them. Besides, it was fun watching the big one puff out his chest.

Locking eyes with my princess, I laid my heart bare, telling the story that had been a long time coming.

"When I returned from seeing you, my father was acting strange. He was trying to put me in situations I didn't want, not listening to me when I said I wasn't interested, and overall, too focused on every move I was making. I knew my time to get Becca out was dwindling. I didn't realize how much until later."

I cleared my throat, shuffling in my seat.

"I was able to finalize a placement through my contact and was to meet him the next day. I went to talk to her and have her pack a bag. That's when she told me she was getting married. The Destroyer had convinced her it was her duty to the club. The man was three times her age and a notorious abuser," I spat, the memory of that night filling me with rage.

"Becca is Maddox's younger sister. She has Down syndrome and has been isolated her whole life in the club."

I nodded, thankful Darcie had given me time to calm down.

"One of the projects Destroyer had me on was to secure a new supplier," I paused, looking at the others, realizing they wouldn't know who the Chaos Gargoyles were. "My father's club dealt primarily in drugs and dabbled in guns. He told me there was a new merchant, and I needed to vet them. Since I'd returned, he'd been putting these projects on me, stating he was preparing me to lead in his stead." I shook my head, laughing darkly. "Except, when I arrived at the meet, I was surrounded by law enforcement officers and a truck full of drugs."

"Shit," Darcie cursed, her eyes worried. I smiled, and the concern felt nice.

"Yeah. I realized too late he'd known I was working

with Tank to take him down. When I was arrested, I used my get-out-of-jail card to save Becca. I hated to leave you, Princess, but it was my only hope to help her."

She nodded, wiping a tear that fell. "It was the right call. Becca needed you. I'm glad she's safe."

The rock I'd been carrying all these years shifted, the guilt lessening at not being able to return to her like I'd promised.

"From there, time seemed to stand still. Prison life wasn't easy, especially when people learned who I was. It took me a while to show I wasn't interested in running any gangs inside. I made some allies with guards and other prisoners, keeping myself safe enough for where I was. When I earned my internet privileges, I reached out to some of the Mavericks' contacts, hoping they could get me out. I thought about reaching out to you every day, but I didn't want to lead anyone to where you were. The hope of finding you again one day was what kept me surviving each miserable day."

"How did you get out?" Darcie asked. "Chase told me you were in prison and that a deal was coming. He wanted me to tell you not to take it."

I sat up, curious about this new information. "Did he say why?"

She shook her head. "No. But he wasn't very forthcoming after I stabbed him and ran."

"Good girl," I said, smiling.

"I looked for you when I got here. Brooks showed me

how to search the prison database. It said that you'd been released. I worried it meant you wouldn't come to find me."

My fingers flexed; the urge to hold her while we had this conversation was strong. But since I was outnumbered, I wanted to respect the dynamics of the group I'd walked into.

"A man came to see me. He wouldn't tell me his name, just that he had an offer for me. If I did the two things he wanted, he'd expunge my record, and I'd be free to live my life."

"And if you didn't?" the prettiest of the three guys asked. I'd already forgotten his name.

I smirked, sitting back and folding my arms over my chest. It was easier to be an asshole when I wasn't staring at Darcie.

"I made sure that nothing would fall back on me if I couldn't fulfill his demand. I'll return to prison and finish out my sentence. A nice white-collared prison at that."

"That's too good of a deal for the price not to be steep," the angry one said. Darcie nodded as well, agreeing with him.

"What do you have to do, Maddox?"

Exhaling, I dropped my arms. "Hand over my father and... Stanley Driscoll."

"Hand over, how?" She sucked in a breath.

"They've been collecting evidence on them. They

only needed one thing for my father." I swallowed as the memory of the past month rushed through my mind. "It wasn't easy, but I managed to do it. It's why it took me so long to come here. I had to secure my father, or I would've never made it out of Georgia."

She sat up, her eyes wide. "Your father, is he... *dead*?"

"No. As much as I wanted to make him suffer, I gave him over to Agent Bones."

"What are you going to do? Will he come after you?" she asked, her voice soft.

"I haven't thought that far ahead yet if I'm honest. I just knew I needed to find you before my next steps. So, here I am."

Her eyes warmed, and she smiled, holding my gaze for a long moment. Glancing up, she caught the big one's eyes. "What do you think?"

The redheaded man watched her, debating something in his mind. He glanced over at the other two, waiting for them to give him something. When he was satisfied, he exhaled and looked at me.

"What are your intentions with Darcie? Are you just a friend, or do you plan to steal her away in the middle of the night and go on the run?"

I had to give it to the man. He had balls to ask me that.

I glanced at Darcie, her eyes sparkling. She was so sure about these men that I would be too.

"Darcie has always been the beat of my heart. I don't

know how not to love her. I'll be in her life in whatever capacity she allows. I'd never assume to know what she needed more than she did. If she chooses you three, I honor that choice and respect her decision, regardless of where that leaves me. Does that answer your question?" I asked, smirking. I just couldn't help poking the bear.

He grunted, a smile curving up one side of his face. "It suffices for now. Do you have a place to stay?"

"The only things I have are the clothes on my back and my bike. Everything else was lost. I was only able to recover the low rider because it had been impounded. Another perk from Agent Bones."

"Then you can stay with us," the pretty one said. "Sunflower doesn't have much need for her bed these days."

If he thought it would enrage me to hear they were sleeping with her, he was in for a surprise. "Perfect. I could use a night of sleep where I didn't have to keep one eye open."

"I wouldn't be so sure about that," the friendly one chided, smiling.

"Touche," I said with a chuckle.

"I'll take Maddox back to the house and get him settled in," Darcie offered, attempting to stand from her perch. The pretty one's arms tightened on her for a second before releasing her. It felt nice that they still thought of me as a threat. It made me believe I still had a chance.

"Cowboy, go with," the big one ordered as we all stood.

The friendly one nodded, not dropping his smile.

"I'm sorry; what were all your names again? I was so excited about finding Princess that everything else faded. I'd like to move on from the pretty one, the friendly one, and the big one."

The room was quiet for a second before they erupted into laughter.

"I guess I'm the friendly one?" the guy in front of me asked, wiping his eyes once he stopped.

"Yeah."

"I'm Brooks or Cowboy. Grayson is the pretty one, also known as Pretty Boy, and the big one is Bubba to most, Waylon to a few."

"You can call me Bubba. You have to earn, Waylon," he muttered, crossing his arms. Despite his attitude, I could tell it was all for show. He just wanted me to believe he was angrier than he was. If he'd protected Darcie from the men trying to find her, then I'd let him have this one.

"Got it. And thanks for letting me crash. It means a lot. I'm glad that Darcie has had you three, honestly."

The guys nodded, taking my thanks to heart.

Later that night, as we sat around a firepit in the backyard, eating hamburgers and drinking a few beers, I imagined a future I'd long given up. One that included a club full of men who were more than members, but brothers, and a woman at the center uniting them.

Perhaps after everything was done, I could finally live a life that wasn't on the run.

My phone vibrated, a message from Agent Bones to not dally here, as I still had to deliver the Agonizer.

It was then I remembered it was a nice dream, but it would never be my future. But for now, I'd pretend, soaking up the time I spent with my princess.

Diary #17

Dear Dad,

Maddox has returned to me. I think I'm still shocked about it, if I'm being honest. I keep looking at him, expecting him to disappear, only a figment of my desperate imagination.

But he's here with me.

The guys aren't sure about him yet, not that I blame them. He's someone new, someone they've only known to leave me.

I'm hoping over time that will change, and they will trust him as much as I do.

Everything I've learned about myself in the last month or so, and all the pain that Maddox has endured, has made me think about things differently.

I'm finally ready to heal and move past things

that should've never happened. And that means it's time to forgive you.

While you played a part in the things that occurred, you weren't responsible for the sick things he did, and I can see that now.

It was easier to be mad at you because I missed you, and it hurt too much. My anger covered the parts that hurt.

I've met some men who fill me with happiness and love. They see me as the strong woman I want to be. Their belief in me has encouraged me to face the hard things.

I'm not sure what will happen now, but I know I'm done hiding.

Love,

Darcie

CHAPTER 18

Darcie

OVER THE NEXT WEEK, things fell into a natural routine. Maddox would join me wherever I worked for the day, getting to know the guys better in the process. He'd easily won over Brooks and Grayson. It was cute how close they'd gotten in the short time frame.

I hadn't ever seen Maddox have a guy friend before, considering he'd always been one of the youngest Mavericks and spent most of his time with my father. Getting to see him bond with two of the guys I'd fallen in love with warmed my heart more than I realized it would.

Bubba hadn't been as quick, and I wondered if it had more to do with protecting me or his stubbornness. He was folding in small ways, giving me hope that he'd come around eventually and accept Maddox as a brother.

Nothing physical had developed between Maddox and me yet. In some ways, I needed more from him before I gave him my body again. But mostly, I wanted the guys to accept him fully, honoring the bonds I've built with them.

As I watched Brooks and Maddox work on a car together, it felt like this was possible. That this could be my life.

Grayson peeked his head into the office, pulling me from my daydreaming. He smiled, setting off the butterflies that had taken up residence in my chest.

"Hey, Sunflower, can you pick up lunch? I thought I'd be able to get away, but the call with the tire representative is in ten minutes."

"Yeah, no problem. Anything in particular?" I asked, standing from the desk.

"I called it into that Chinese place you like so much." He winked, walking closer to pull me into his arms.

"This feels like a bribe," I teased.

"Me? I'd never stoop to such measures to get you into my bed. I'm a man of honor."

Giggling, my eyes felt like they were leaking emotion all over the man. "You keep telling yourself that, Pretty Boy. You're all tease."

He bent down, whispering low into my ear. "I thought you liked it when I made you come so hard your legs shook? Or was I mistaken?" Grayson lifted his eyes, daring me to say no.

"Yes, well, that has nothing to do with honor," I said, trying to recover. My pussy throbbed from his words, the ache growing the longer he looked at me.

"I promise to *honor* you with several orgasms. How about that?"

I cleared my throat, nodding. "Yeah, that could work."

He smiled, leaning down to kiss me. "Hurry back."

Taking the keys from his outstretched hand, I waved to the others as I headed outside. Shielding my eyes, I hurried to the truck and lifted myself up into it. I'd gotten more comfortable driving the machine since I'd been with the guys. But I still preferred my bike. The thought of carrying containers of Chinese food while driving wasn't a good one, though, so I'd suck it up and use the truck.

The garage wasn't far from the strip mall I'd gone to the first day. I pulled in, avoiding the pawn shop. That place still gave me the creeps.

Parking a little closer, I hurried across the lot toward the restaurant. My stomach growled when I walked in, the smells sending me into a hunger frenzy.

"Hi," I chirped when I spotted the kind woman from my first visit.

"It's you!" She smiled, waving me forward. "How have you been?"

"I've been great. Thanks again for looking out for me that day. It was very kind."

She waved me off, her cheeks heating. "Same order?" she asked.

"Actually, a call-in order for PB Mechanics."

"Oh, he is a very nice man. Good tipper." She winked

before walking back to grab the bags of food. "Good choice."

Laughing, I thanked her and took the food from her, promising to come back with Grayson someday. I wondered what she'd think if she knew I was with three guys.

Smiling, I waved as I headed out the door laden with two bags of food. Walking carefully, I focused on each step I took as I approached the truck. A chill ran down my back, and I looked up, searching it out. Nothing stood out, but I quickened my pace, wanting to get back to my guys.

Tossing the food into the backseat, I climbed in and pulled out, barely stopping to put my seatbelt on. Once I was out of the parking lot, my heart slowed, my chest easing the further I drove. I didn't get far when the truck tilted, a grinding sound filling the space.

"Shit," I cursed, pulling off to a side road. Climbing out, I grabbed my phone and called Bubba since Grayson had his work call. He answered in one ring, making me smile.

"My Queen," he said, his voice soft and husky.

"I love when you call me that," I said, smiling. "So listen, it's probably nothing, but the truck made a weird sound when I left the Chinese restaurant. I pulled off onto that side road. Can you come and check it out? I don't want to drive it more if something's wrong." I walked around the front, looking at the tires. When I got to the rear one, I saw what was wrong.

"Actually, I found out what's wrong. Looks like I ran over some metal or something. Shit."

"I'm on my way. Wait in the truck."

"Yes, sir."

"I mean it, Darcie." His voice was serious, making me instantly go on alert.

"Okay, I'm heading there now." I turned, freezing in my tracks. I sucked in a breath as I met the eyes of the man from the pawnshop.

"Give me that," he ordered, taking my phone and crushing it beneath his foot. I'd heard Bubba shouting my name, so I prayed he heard the man as well.

My body shook as fear threatened to take over. The man from the pawnshop sneered, licking his lips.

"I knew you were trash when you walked into my store. I've been waiting for the perfect opportunity to show you what happens to sluts like you." He grabbed me and pulled me under his arm. He bent down to sniff my neck. "When I saw the bounty on your head, I knew it was fate. I've been trying to find ways to grab you, but you're always with those men, whoring yourself."

"You were at the bar. Weren't you? You've been following me," I said, the sound weak even to my own ears.

"Do you really think I couldn't track you through a device I sold you?"

It explained the weird sensation I had a few times when I'd been out with the guys. But until today, I hadn't been alone.

"Finally, I got you alone and knew I had to act fast. Damaging your tire was easy, but hiding in the back was my favorite. You never knew I was there." He laughed, the sound sending shivers through me. I did not want to be his captive. "You're worth a lot of money, slut. Thankfully, it doesn't say what condition you have to be in. Just alive. So, I'm going to have some fun with you first, then I'll hand you over for my reward."

The man groped my breast, squeezing it hard as he licked my neck. The fear fell away at his words, and my anger emerged. Blind rage filled my mind. I refused to let another man decide my fate. Nor would he take anything from me I wasn't freely giving.

"Not today, asshole," I screamed, rearing my head back at the same time I shoved my elbow into his gut. He bent over, dropping his hold on me. I didn't hesitate as I took off running toward the cornfield. Bubba was on his way. I knew it. I just needed to hide long enough for him to arrive.

The cornstalks slapped my face as I ran, blinding me. My mind raced as I tried to pinpoint which direction the shop was in. If I had to, I'd run there and let Bubba deal with that piece of shit.

The engine of a bike roared close, and I stopped, bending at the waist as I caught my breath. A body tackled me, my face smacking into the dirt. Their weight pressed down on me, and I struggled to breathe. Whimpering, I hated how weak I sounded. This wasn't who I was anymore.

The warrior I'd been groomed to be my whole life rose up in me, giving me the strength to keep fighting.

"I said *no*. Learn about consent, douchebag."

"I'm going to teach you to shut up first," he sneered, pressing his knees into my back. He pulled at my hair, yanking my head up. Spitting out dirt and blood, my body tingled from the hit, but I wouldn't let it stop me.

Wetness hit me right before the weight was lifted. I coughed, rolling over to see what had happened. The creepy asshole held his neck where he was bleeding from a wound. He looked shocked, surprised to see his own blood.

Glancing past him, I expected to see Bubba, a smile already spreading across my face. Instead, a face I never expected to see again stared at me with wide eyes.

"Damon?" I asked, despite knowing it was him. My head hurt, and I wondered if I'd hit it hard enough to get a concussion.

His hands shook, a knife covered in blood in one of his palms. "I didn't... I didn't mean to," he stuttered.

Pulling myself off the ground, I stood, my body aching. "It's okay, Damon. You saved me."

His eyes met mine, and he looked me over as he repeated what I said. "I saved you. Yes, you're right. I didn't have a choice. You needed me."

I disagreed with him, but I nodded, wanting to get out of this cornfield.

"Not that I'm not thankful, Damon, but what are you doing here?"

His eyes met mine, something shifting as he stared. "I came to get you. You need my help, Darcie."

I stepped back, not liking what he was saying. "Damon, I'm fine. While I appreciate you stepping in, I'm okay now."

"No, you're not." His voice was hard now.

Quicker than I imagined possible, he grabbed me and dragged me out in the other direction. The knife pressed into my side, stopping all thoughts of running.

"Damon, this isn't you. We can talk. What's going on?"

"I can't stop thinking about you, Darcie. All day. All night. I can't work because all I do is think about you. I realized I'd made a mistake when I walked away. We do belong together. But then you were gone. I waited at your apartment for weeks. When they packed up your belongings, I knew you'd run, too sad to live without me. I thought I'd never find you again, destined to live alone and miserable. But then my brother told me he ran into you with that rodeo guy. I knew it was a message. You wanted me to come and rescue you. It's a good thing I did too. Why was that guy chasing you?"

My head spun as he talked, trying to sort it out. His words were so fast, they didn't make sense. None of this day was making sense.

"I'm sorry you can't find a job, Damon, but I'm not yours. I belong only to myself. Besides, you made your feelings clear when you said I had to choose only you.

Call me whatever you want, but my heart is big enough to love more than one person."

"You're just saying that. You love me. I know it. They've convinced you to be their club whore. But you're better than that," he cooed like he was talking to a baby.

I shook my head, tired of his nonsense. "It doesn't matter. I don't have feelings for you. Damon, I've moved on. I'm sorry if that's not what you want to hear, but I don't want to be with you."

Damon growled, his grip tightening on me. "You just need to get away from them. Then you'll be able to think clearly. I know this is what you want."

"No," I shouted, fed up with this argument.

Damon yanked me, my feet clearing the other side of the cornfield as I tilted toward the ground. The knife dug into me, pricking my skin as his grip slipped with my momentum. I spotted his old pickup truck parked on the dirt path, fear gnawing at me. I couldn't get into his vehicle. There would be no way for the guys to find me if I did.

Deciding to take my chances with his knife, I used all my body weight to fall to the ground, pulling him with me. The blade pierced me; the pain of it burning as he fell on top of me. Okay, that might've been the worst idea I'd ever had.

Ignoring the pain, I scrambled back, pushing him away with my feet. "Stay the fuck away from me," I screamed, praying that one of the guys was here by now and would hear. Pressing my hand down on the wound, I kept pressure as I continued to move back in a crab walk. I couldn't stop. I wouldn't.

Damon grunted, getting to his knees. His eyes lifted, spitting fire as he looked at me from head to toe. He prowled closer, a sneer covering his face, the knife still held in his hand. It was coated in blood now—mine and the creep's. Shit, I hope he didn't have any bloodborne diseases.

I kept moving, not willing to stop, even if it was only an inch at a time. I grabbed a handful of dirt and threw it in his face when he neared.

"Fucking hell, Darcie. Why are you fighting me so much?"

"Because I don't want to go with you. How much clearer do I need to say it?"

My heart pounded in my ears, my blood pumping hard as adrenaline and fear coursed through my body. I just had to hang on a little longer. They'd come for me. I knew it.

Damon stood up again; dirt and blood smeared all over. His once handsome face distorted as he sneered at me, obsession and hatred flashing in his eyes. He didn't love me. He just wanted to conquer me to say he had. I was nothing but a trophy for him to win.

The world spun as my vision grew blurry. Shit, I couldn't lose consciousness.

"I bet your pussy isn't even worth all this trouble," he spat, looking down at me.

Despite my hope to keep moving, it seemed I'd reached my limit.

"You're right. I'm not. Just leave, and I'll forget all about this. I promise."

He stalled, and I hoped he was thinking it over.

"I'd do what she said if I were you," a menacing voice said, my heart lifting.

I knew that voice. It meant I could let go now. That I wasn't alone anymore.

My eyes fluttered closed, the sound of a scuffle occurring in the distance. Hands gripped me, and I whimpered until soft lips brushed against my forehead.

"I got you, Princess. Just stay with me."

It was the last thing I needed to hear before I fell into the black hole I'd been circling.

Dear Lennox,

Once again, you saved me.

Or your father did this time.

Bubba told me how he called your dad when I was taken, telling him who I was. Or a version of that. He kept my name out of the report, helping me to stay hidden. I know that couldn't have been easy for him to do, so tell your dad thanks the next time he calls you.

Damon was taken into custody and charged with killing the creepy guy. I still can't believe he'd tried to kidnap me. Maddox told me his face was barely recognizable when Bubba was done with him. I wanted to feel bad for Damon, but since he stabbed and almost killed me, I'm not feeling all that charitable.

The best thing about my attempted abduction was Bubba and Maddox becoming buds. They worked together to rescue me, bonding them together for life, apparently. Who knew that was all I needed to do?

Though, I do not recommend trying that. Results may vary.

As scary as the whole thing was, I feel stronger. I fought against them, buying myself time until others could get there.

It showed me I don't have to hide anymore.

I'm done running.

The guys have shown me that I'm their queen, and there's nothing I can't do with them by my side.

So with that, it's time to return home, face my father, and take down the Agonizer. My dad groomed me to take over the Mavericks one day, and I'm finally ready to claim my legacy.

Instead of a Pres, they're going to get a Queen.

I hope they're prepared, because this chick is ready to ride.

Love,

Your Darcie

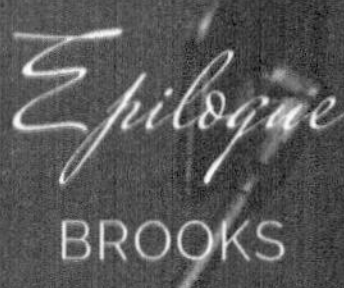

Epilogue

BROOKS

MY EYES STAYED GLUED to Darcie as she talked with Grayson and Maddox. It had become a necessity after she'd been hurt. I needed to ensure she was safe at all times. I still couldn't wrap my head around the fact I'd almost lost her... twice.

When Bubba had called, Maddox took off without a second thought, ready to dive into danger for her. Grayson was only a few steps behind him when he noticed me.

I was frozen to the spot, my face white as a ghost. *I couldn't lose her.* But my fear made me incapable of stopping it.

By the time Grayson had calmed me down, we arrived on the scene to watch her being taken away in an ambulance. Waylon was dealing with the cops and sent us to the hospital. I went willingly, needing to prove my worth in the relationship and verify she was okay.

Since that day three weeks ago, I hadn't been able to let her out of my sight, or I'd break out into a cold sweat if I didn't know she was with the others. I needed to get my shit together, and fast. I would be useless to her otherwise.

"Nope. Put it back," Darcie teased, slapping Grayson's hand as he tried to shove something into another bag.

They were going over the last of the supplies we needed. Waylon had also wanted to take the truck, but no one was willing to give up their bike to do it. So, in the end, we had to take only what we could carry.

Of course, for Grayson, that was turning out to be a challenging task.

"But I need it," he whined, giving her his puppy dog look.

"No one needs four different types of shampoo and hair gel," Darcie said, smiling at him. Grayson huffed, preparing to argue his point.

Maddox watched them, shaking his head at their antics as he rolled up his last shirt. He had the easiest task, since he didn't have that much to begin with. He looked up and caught my eyes, searching them for a moment. Closing his saddlebag, he walked over and leaned against the workbench I was at.

"What's on your mind, Cowboy? Are you thinking about our journey?"

I nodded, dropping my eyes to turn and organize the

tools. It was a ridiculous effort to avoid talking, but I tried anyway.

"I wish I could tell you that the world we're about to enter was safe, but I can't. Plus, I'd be doing you a disservice if I did. I don't want to insult you by saying you can stay here. I know you won't consider it because I'd never be able to either. Long ago, I learned that promises mean nothing when it comes to ruthless men willing to do whatever it takes to keep their empire."

He turned more, so our conversation was kept from the others. He waited until I looked up and could speak directly to me.

"I'm not going to promise we'll all be okay or make it through this. There's too much that I've seen and I've fought my way through hell and back for that girl, but I can say *this* with utter conviction. I will do everything in my power to protect our girl, even give my own life." Maddox paused, glancing back at the woman who'd stolen our hearts. "She's strong. She's ready to face this. Darcie's trained and grown into a true queen. *She's* the true threat. These men we'll be facing will be blindsided by her. I'm not saying not to worry, but have faith in her and us. Yourself included."

I wanted to believe him, but I'd already failed at being there for her.

"I'm not like you. I froze last time. So I'm just going to get in the way. But even knowing that, I can't seem to let her go."

"Brooks, I'm not one for pep talks. I'm just going to say it how it is, okay?"

I nodded, bracing myself.

"How would you describe Darcie?" he asked, surprising me.

"Um, beautiful, kind, endearing, and strong. She's overcome so much, and I want to shield her from any more pain."

"Would someone like that love a man who 'just gets in the way'?"

He narrowed his eyes at me, waiting for me to answer. I gaped, realizing what he'd done by using my own words against me.

"No, but that doesn't mean I'm the best one for this."

"You're the best one for this because she chose you. If you want to shield her from pain, then get out of your own head and see the life waiting for you to live. If you don't, you will do exactly what you don't want to do. Hurt her. And to me, that's a greater fault than not being just like me. She doesn't need another me. She needs you, man."

His words hit like a slap across the face, and I knew he was right. I was the one creating my own obstacles by being insecure and afraid.

"How do I deal with the fear?" I asked, standing straighter.

"Use it instead of letting *it* use you. How you do that

will be for you to decide." He turned, leaning against the toolbox again, staring at Darcie with a smile on his face.

I joined him, letting all the words he'd said sink in. I'd been stuck on the fear, unsure how to deal with it, letting it consume me.

Being afraid wasn't a new concept to me. I'd been afraid of most things my whole life. But I'd also learned to conquer them.

When I couldn't talk to my peers, I learned how to ride a horse, finding security and strength in the animals. Eventually, I grew confident in my ability and found a passion that led me to the rodeo. For eight seconds on the back of a bucking horse, I made fear my bitch.

I overcame my shyness with girls by practicing online. It helped me find a way to be myself without changing who I was. I gained the courage to try something new, leading me to meet and fall in love with Darcie.

Not having a family, I always wanted to belong some-where. Meeting the guys, I gained brothers to support me and encourage me. I wasn't alone anymore.

Taking a deep breath, I felt my body relax at the knowledge, reminding me how I'd found my own way every time. It didn't look like your typical journey, but it was mine.

Being scared wasn't new, so I just needed to find a way to tackle this for myself.

"Thank you. I'll work on it. I'll find my path."

Maddox turned and wrapped an arm around me,

squeezing my shoulder. The embrace felt nice, easing some of the fear out of me.

"I know I'm the new guy, but I'm here for you, man. If there's something I can help you with, then let me know, and I will. I trained Darcie, so I can train you too, if you want."

"That might be helpful. It will give me something to focus on, if nothing else."

Maddox grinned, his eyes slanting with the motion. Something told me I might regret asking him, but I couldn't deny it would be nice to feel stronger and more prepared.

"We'll start when we stop next. Now, let's grab those two before we're late for our appointment. Bubba will ground us all then, and we'd get nowhere."

Chuckling, I walked over with Maddox to Grayson and Darcie as they kissed against his bike. I already felt lighter and knew I owed Maddox for talking me off the ledge.

"Hey, lovebirds, we have an appointment to keep," Maddox shouted, breaking them apart.

Darcie frowned at being stopped until Maddox's words registered. Her eyes lit up, and she gave a little happy dance as she looked at us.

"It's time?" she asked.

Nodding, I reached out to her. Little moments like this made me realize how much I missed her. I'd been unnecessarily holding myself back as a form of punishment.

She easily took my hand, falling into my arms as she grinned at me. This was what I needed to focus on. Not what I couldn't give her, but what I did.

All four of us climbed into the truck with Grayson driving. The drive to the shop was quiet as we fell into silence. The parking lot was empty since it was Sunday afternoon, and most businesses were closed. Waylon had come in earlier to prepare for his departure. He'd talked with Slade, and they'd hired a temporary assistant to cover the shop while he was gone.

I knew it had to be hard for him to step away when he felt Slade was counting on him to man the store. But when Darcie needed him, Waylon didn't blink when it came to a decision for us all to go with her.

Stepping into the tattoo shop, I swallowed some nerves, focusing on what this next step would represent.

"Waylon!" Darcie shouted, practically skipping as she entered. "I want to go first."

He stepped out from the back office, a grin peeking out between his beard. "You sure about that, baby?"

"Yep. I'm ready." She flopped down into the chair, turning her forearm over. Waylon sat down, pulling on his gloves as he got ready to work. The rest of us stood back to watch, and I wondered if they were as nervous as I was for my turn. I didn't do well with needles, but for Darcie and them, I would suck it up and deal with it. This was an important step, after all.

When Darcie had told us about the bounty on her head and her decision to return home to face her father and the man that had sent her running, we knew we couldn't let her go alone. She told us her plan to claim her legacy instead of hiding from it, tired of running from the past.

It wasn't a question of joining her, but more of what it meant for us as a whole. It didn't feel right to join the Mavericks, a club that had let Darcie down when she needed them the most. But the Brotherhood no longer fit either. We'd become more than that.

"Done," Waylon said, wiping it before he put on some cream and gently wrapped her forearm.

Grayson went next, turning over the same wrist, not even caring that he was marring his skin and ruining potential modeling jobs. Darcie was more important than that.

Soon, Grayson was done, and Maddox went, leaving me standing as I watched. Even Waylon already had the mark; another artist had given it to him earlier today. I bit my lip as my foot bounced, my nerves coming to the forefront.

Darcie walked over, placing her hand on my knee. "If you don't want to do it, it's okay. I know you don't like needles."

I shook my head. "I'm doing it. It's important."

She kissed my cheek, stepping back so I could take my place in the seat. Sucking in a deep breath, I hurried over, focusing on everything else but what Waylon was doing.

I barely remembered breathing as the needle pierced

my skin, my hand gripping the other side of the chair. It wasn't until Darcie unfolded my fingers, taking my hand in hers, that I calmed. When it was over, I let out a huge breath, my lungs filling with oxygen as I remembered to breathe.

I glanced down at the tattoo that now resembled our group—a black outline of a crown with an R in the middle.

We were more than just the Brotherhood and the Mavericks; we were a family. A beautiful unity centered around one woman—our queen—merging to bring a new group into existence.

The Royals—united in blood, bonded in love.

With a sole focus of protecting our woman. Together, we were unstoppable, and that was a beautifully dangerous thing.

It was time for the Agonizer to pay for his sins and bow down to the Queen.

There was no escaping. The Royals were coming.

Those last few chapters were intense! Darcie's story started rough, and she had a lot of things she had to work through, but our sassy and fun-loving bestie of Lennox is taking her stand, and she's got four hot guys behind her.

These men... I loved Bubba from Lennox's story, so I was so happy when he got to meet Darcie and fall in love. That teddy bear ginger needs some love. Cowboy is too sweet for words, and Pretty Boy will swoon you right off your feet. And then there's Maddox. He's so understanding and accepting of where she's at in her life and what she needs. It will be fun to see how his and Bubba's alphadog energy measure up together once they get on the road.

There will be one more book in Darcie's story, Beautiful Unity. I hope to get it out by the end of the year, but if not, then it will be early next year. Our sassy queen needs her happy ending.

Thank you for reading and loving these characters. I'm so grateful to the team around me and the readers who have picked up my books.

Emma, Megan, and Heather—thank you for being my sounding board and fighting over who licks who, even though we know all the tatts go to Megan. Lindsay and Kayla—you girls rock so hard and are always willing to dive in when I need you. So, thank you.

To my Arc readers, I'm so glad you wanted to continue Darcie's story even though there's been a year in between. It makes me happy to see how much love she has.

If you're a new reader, check out Lennox's series, Tattooed Hearts, and meet Bubba and Darcie, or pick up any of my other books. There's something for every mood.

Happy Reading!
Love, Kris

THE ORDER DUET (COUNCIL SPINOFF)

#secret agency #spy + hacker games #fashionista

4 guys, light MM (book 2 only at the end)

Stiletto Sins

Lipstick Lies

DRESSED TO KILL SHARED WORLD (STANDALONE)

#female assassin #quirky & curvy #twins

4 guys, no MM

Raven

F*CK STEAL KILL (STANDALONE)

#morally gray #bestie unalivers #sassy

3 guys, biawakening

F*ck Steal Kill

DARK CONFESSIONS (COMPLETED)

#mafia #therapist #foster kids + dogs #tattoos

5 guys with MM

Dangerous Truths

Dangerous Lies

Dangerous Vows

Reckless (Cami's Novella)

Relentless (Nat's Novella)

Dangerous Love

TATTOOED HEARTS DUET (COMPLETED)

#tattoos #penpals #music #curvy fmc

3 guys with MM

Riddled Deceit (Part 1)

Smudged Lines (Part 2)

Open Road (Road trip Novella)

Tattooed Hearts Completed Duet

MUSIC CITY DIARIES (TATTOOED HEARTS SPIN-OFF)

#motorcycle club #age gap #TW #cam girl

4 guys, no MM

Beautiful Agony

Beautiful Envy

VACATION ROMCOM

#romcom #social media experiment #besties

3 guys, no MM

Vibing

SINNERS FAIRYTALES (STANDALONE)

#Rapunzel retelling #dance #TW

3 guys, no MM

Pride

Kris Butler writes under a pen name to have some separation from her everyday life. Writing has become her second love, providing a safe place to normalize mental health through her characters.

Kris enjoys writing emotional books with flawed characters, sassy heroines, and all the book boyfriends she loves to drool over.

You can find her at home most nights reading with her husband and furbaby, trying to maintain her nerdy sock collection, or playing tabletop games with her friends. Kris loves to talk with readers about her books, even if it's just them yelling at her for that cliffhanger.

If you enjoyed her book, please consider leaving a review. You can find her in her reader group or on social media.

Join my <u>newsletter</u>
Join my <u>fan group</u>
Check out my <u>website</u>

www.ingramcontent.com/pod-product-compliance
Lightning Source LLC
Chambersburg PA
CBHW032018310726
48972CB00002B/452